Envy

SEVEN DEADLY SINS

Compiled & Edited by
Ben Thomas & D Kershaw

Also available from Black Hare Press

DARK DRABBLES ANTHOLOGIES

WORLDS
ANGELS
MONSTERS
BEYOND
UNRAVEL
APOCALYPSE
LOVE
HATE
OCEANS
ANCIENTS

BHP WRITERS' GROUP SPECIAL EDITIONS

STORMING AREA 51
EERIE CHRISTMAS
BAD ROMANCE
TWENTY TWENTY

OTHER VOLUMES

DEEP SEA
WHAT IF?
KEY TO THE KINGDOM
BEYOND THE REALM

Twitter: @BlackHarePress
Facebook: BlackHarePress
Website: www.BlackHarePress.com

A shuddering deluge whelmed your wake of yore:

You razed the halls of fatal Paris' sire:

Loaded the dice of Actium : lit the fire

Changing pale Magian to the Scarlet Whore,

Who Phrygian swine and Messalina bore,

And sterile spouses of the modern mire:

Your undertone jangles the lyric choir:

Your furtive fingers smear the lover's lore.

Mandrake, disgorged by grave of murdered Shame,

Clinging to dozing Trust with vampire lips,

Oily with fetid Sodom, or the wan

Gomorrah-sin the ages dare not name!

Seductive wrecker of immortal ships!

Serpent of Eden! Brothel toad! Begone! 10 II.

Envy **by Bernard O'Dowd, 1909**

Table of Contents

by K.B. Elijah

Outside, there's nothing but blackness, a darkness so absolute that if the human mind could stand it, it would conjure false images to fill the void. Stars, perhaps, burning beacons of light that appear close enough to touch. Other ships passing by—a freighter maybe, or a colony transport vessel.

But there's nothing. Not here, in this corner of eternity.

Space is vast. If a ship can travel for weeks without seeing another on the oceans of the Earth, why couldn't one travel for years across the galaxy without an encounter?

But if the outside is cold, bitter, and empty, the inside offers a cheery juxtaposition, at least at first glance. Soft music winds its way through the corridors—an upbeat tune that was all the rage when he left Earth but is likely outdated now. They don't care. They like it.

Marisse hums under her breath, her crayons scribbling strong beads of waxy colour onto the page. They're worn down to the stubs, and Elvin should stop her, should conserve their brightness for another day, but he doesn't. So what if the crayons run out? They've seen Marisse through her childhood, and there're no other kids on board. If the time comes for Marisse to have her own children and they still haven't reached Earth, then they would have bigger problems than a lack of crayons. A father to create these impossible children, for one.

So, Elvin doesn't stop her, not even as she makes careless scrawls across multiple pieces of precious paper, ruining them. Again, she's the only one who would ever use paper; everything he does is digital. Sometimes he longs for something in his hands, a way to craft like the artisans of old, rather than everything being controlled by the tip of a finger. Was that how we were meant to lead, he wonders, at the furthest end of our limbs? As far away from the heart and mind as we can get?

He's prodding at the chessboard now, wishing he could wrap his fingers around the pieces. But they're nothing but a hologram, a digital manifestation of what he was told was once a work of art.

"Marisse," he says softly from his chair, forlorn hope written into his voice. He knows what her answer will be. "Are you sure you don't want to learn chess?"

She sticks her tongue out at him without looking up. "Chess is silly, daddy. The horses can't go where they want to go."

"The knights move where they're supposed to," he corrects, but she only wrinkles her nose.

"Horses should be free. They should be able to run around and gobble everyone up and win the game."

Horses should be free. Elvin gazes at the back of her head sadly. *Oh daughter, my heart will break the day you realise that you are more a prisoner than they, unable to take a foot outside this ship as I have been unable to do so for more than a decade. I wish you could go wherever you wanted, too, but as chess rules bind the knight, so do life's rules bind us.*

"I'll play with you," offers Evie, the third member of their family. Her harsh voice echoes through the speakers next to Elvin's head, and he winces.

"No thanks, Evie. It's no better than playing myself."

"But you're playing against me!" she whines and something inside of him growls in frustration. He'd never made her this pathetic.

"I have to move all the pieces myself," Elvin says, but that isn't the real reason. He could have easily hooked the chessboard into the mainframe a long time ago, allowed Evie to manipulate the holographic pieces as easily as him. He sighs, realising he owes her the truth. "I programmed you. I know the moves you'll make, because they're mine. Forget it."

"What if I play as Marisse?" Evie suggests, her voice suddenly expelling from another speaker so it is directed to the child on the floor.

Marisse gives her the same wrinkled nose as a few moments before, the same uncaring but fond disdain. "Nuh-uh," she says. "It feels funny when you take over me like that."

"Agreed," Elvin affirms. "No more AI possession. It's creepy seeing my daughter move like a different person."

And it hurts in a different way, he thinks. *I'm jealous of her, being able to touch eternity like that, feel the whisper of power. I made you. You're mine.*

"I just want to play!" Evie complains, but he rises, stretching, nudging the chessboard's display off with his thumb.

"I'm going for a run," Elvin announces, his heart sinking at the thought of jogging through the same corridors he's stared at for the last ten years. Maybe he'll permit himself to mix things up a day early, do his anti-clockwise circuit today instead of tomorrow. "Keep an eye on the navigation for me, E.V.I.E.?"

***

Evie watches the man leave the room. Watches him move to his pod, get changed.

Watches him start jogging around the circumference of the ship with a morose look on his face.

Elvin is ungrateful for what he has. A body, an ability to affect the physical, that rush of movement and energy. The chance to change the universe. Why couldn't he realise how lucky he really is?

Evie withdraws to the control centre, musing on a thought that is growing inside her like a warm spark of electricity. There's no need to keep an eye on the navigation: they'd been travelling in the same direction, at the same speed, for years. Back when Marisse had been nothing but a squalling ball of fisted hands and chubby legs. Before that, when Elvin had cast a wrapped parcel through the airlock, weeping bitterly. Further back, when there had been two different humans aboard: Elvin and Frahe, doing strange things to each other in the darkness of their shared pod, a curious sight Evie couldn't help but watch. Back when their eyes had been full of hope, before the second engine failed and their speed dropped to a mere crawl across the galaxy.

She thinks some more, heating the processing units that give her the ability to do so and triggering their fans to spin faster.

Want.

It all came down to want. Human and AI alike—they both wanted something they couldn't have.

Or could they?

Down in the murky depths of the ship, her fans scream with overuse.

***

It takes six weeks, two days, three hours, forty-four minutes, and eleven seconds. If asked, Evie would have said it was too long, but what did she know about time? It was just a number in a system designed to tick through a pre-programmed series of figures at a defined interval.

She doesn't feel it pass, not really.

The actual calculations and system configuration only take half of that period; the remainder taken up by a continuous assessment of Elvin's mood. She may only have one chance at this, and it has to be right.

If Elvin is too depressed, he may not listen at all. If he is too happy, he wouldn't agree.

And finally, on a day that a system in the ship designated as "Wednesday," she sees her chance.

"…it was beautiful," Elvin is saying to Marisse, his fingers idly tracing the shape of the buttons on the dashboard in front of him. His daughter, done with crayons *"forever, daddy!"*, is making a plastic horse with a missing leg prance vertically up a wall. "The power it gave us, the power over a whole world of information. I could search for whatever I wanted, in an instant." He snaps his fingers, the sudden noise echoing around the empty corridors of the ship. Marisse doesn't even look around, clicking her tongue to make the horse climb faster.

The Internet, Evie realises. He's reminiscing about the interconnected network of Earth.

"I feel like that sometimes," she says casually. She usually hates the way her monotone voice doesn't express emotion, but now she's thankful for how it hides the uncertainty in her thoughts. "My systems are so large that it's almost overwhelming, even to me, a mass of wild data. I can project myself across the entire ship instantaneously, taking in every movement, fluctuation, sight, and sound in an instant."

"Mmm," Elvin says.

She needs to make it more enticing.

"If you could have seen that nebula we passed eighteen months ago," she offers slyly. "Oh, I know you pressed yourself to the porthole, looking at it through blurry, foot-thick glass, but I meant really *see* it. Send probes dancing among its beauty, like tentative caresses through space. Understand how it moves, how it will have changed in a thousand years' time, tune your vision to beyond that of a human to see the hidden colours underneath. It was…unforgettable."

And yet she'd forgotten about it until this moment.

"Evie!" Elvin sounds cross. "You know I can't experience those things. Don't rub it in!"

But it was alright for him to complain about how his head hurt, how he'd bumped his shin on a table? She couldn't feel those things, but he sure went on about them, inciting deep wistfulness inside her.

"What if you could?" is all Evie says.

"If you're talking about the AI possession thing…"

"I'm talking about it," she confirms. "But not possession. Switching."

Elvin frowns.

"I've worked it out," Evie adds, as Marisse discards her horse and starts playing with the plastic hay bale that accompanies it, making it shoot around the air like it can fly. Marisse has never seen a hay bale in real life. She doesn't know better.

Evie has never seen a hay bale either. Maybe they can fly.

"I've worked it out," she repeats, wishing again that she could soften her voice. "A way to transfer consciousness between us. You could be eternal, Elvin, just think about it! The system at your control. Everything you ever *wanted*."

"Don't tell me what I want," he snaps, but he can't lie to her. She's seen the long hours he spends poring over schematics and diagrams. She heard the words he whispered to her back in the early days, words of longing and hope and regret. She'd received the messages that Frahe muttered also, less kind and just as honest, about Elvin naming Evie after himself, or at least the part of him that wanted to leave his wife behind and immerse himself into an ocean of data and circuits and science.

Evie had long ruminated on the words, wondering at their truth about her. It never had made sense, calling an artificial intelligence an "Enhanced Virtual Intelligence Entity." "Enhanced" was a pretty poor way of describing how much more she was than a simple VI, an entire system of thought and analysis and feeling. Had Elvin just forced the words to fit the acronym, wanting something mirrored in his image even by name?

"How would you do it?" he asks now, and she tells him. No guile, not here. Besides, she has nothing to hide—she'd crunched the numbers, and it would work.

Elvin never asks whether it would. After all,

she is him, but better. He trusts her because he trusts himself, believes in her for entirely vain and egotistical reasons. But it's still belief.

He opens his mouth, a smile dancing on his lips as if he is going to say yes. But then Marisse lets out a plaintive cry as the hay bale slips from her fingers and falls through the grate at the edge of the room, one which vents heat and air across the ship. Evie feels it come to rest between two pipes on the third level, snug in its nest and stationary, like a hay bale is meant to be.

"What about her?" Elvin asks.

Evie feels a surge of anger. As if he cares!

"I'll take care of her, Elvin. We will look after her, just as we have, but with me to tuck her into bed each night, brush her hair, hold her close when she has nightmares."

Elvin flinches at that, and well he should. He hasn't done any of those things in a long time.

She expects more questions. Why would she agree to this? Doesn't she know that she would be subjecting herself to a mortal's lifespan, a half-used one at that? But they never come. He doesn't care, and it tastes like bitter rust.

"Daddy?" Marisse asks, her eyes wide and lost. "Daddy, are you leaving me?"

Elvin kneels down before her, hands on her shoulders as if she is an adult, not a child of five years old. "I'll still be here, darling. Watching over you. I love you, sweetie."

One kiss pressed to the top of her head, and he is done, standing tall with a determined set to his jaw.

"Daddy, I don't want you to go!" Marisse's voice trembles with fear and want, a dangerous cocktail of emotional manipulation, even if it is bathed in innocence.

But his child's cries have no effect on the man that stands before her, inside her. Marisse's desperate pleas mean nothing, not when she stands in the way of eternal knowledge.

"Do it, Evie. Make the switch."

Evie does, with no more remorse than he. She craves a physical body, needs to touch and feel and hurt. He wants her life, a cold and distant power. They feel the same, Elvin and Evie, a longing for what the other has. What is the true difference between human and AI, when that binds them together so completely?

Enhanced virtual intelligence, indeed. Evie is certainly not virtual now.

Maybe I should change my name, she muses. *Enhanced Non-Virtual Intelligence Entity has a nice ring to it.*

And then reality hits.

Evie takes a deep shuddering breath, a strange, cool lightness flooding her insides. She feels heavy, like she will crash through the floor, but she strains against the sensation, holding herself upright.

"Daddy?" Marisse, so close, so real.

Evie pulls them together with an awkward movement, presses her cheek against the girl's.

"I'm here," she says.

The Envious Eye
by Tim Mendees

Envy is a curious thing, especially when you are a teenager. All those hormones running wild mean that the green-eyed monster is never far from the surface and can be summoned over the pettiest and most inconsequential of reasons.

Rob was part of a small social group of fifteen- to sixteen-year-old rebels. These were the school slackers, smokers, underage drinkers, and skirt chasers. Never the most popular kids nor the outcasts, most of the school looked upon them with a kind of confused awe. These were the lads that never did PE: an exemption note was easy to forge. They never turned up to detentions; Rob used to collect slips—he had hundreds by the time he left. And they never did their homework. They preferred to smoke dope and listen to grunge instead. Every UK school in the early '90s had a group like Rob and his friends.

The biggest event on the social calendar was Saturday afternoons. Where they would meet up, those who hadn't been grounded for rolling in drunk, late, or both on Friday that is, and head into town. Towns are exciting places when you are a teenager, not the soul-sucking ordeal that they become as you get older. The group would spend an hour or two flicking through the local record shop then dedicate the remainder of the afternoon to attempting to pick up girls. Indulging in what Pop Will Eat Itself described in their seminal 1987 classic as "Beaver Patrol."

Once they failed in their mission—and let's face it when your most sophisticated technique is to lick a finger, touch a pretty girl's coat, and say "We had better get you out of those wet clothes," it was inevitable—they headed to George's Cards.

Not merely a card shop, George's was a Mecca to the alternative crowd of Betyls Cove. George stocked an eclectic mixture of occult and spiritual paraphernalia, everything from pentagrams and crystals to incense, ceremonial daggers, and strange herbal medicines. This wasn't the big draw either. The big draw was the wide range of "adult gifts," everything from inflatable sex sheep to chocolate willies, you name it; if it was rude and hilarious, George stocked it.

Magic Eye pictures were all the rage back then; the concept was simple; you stared at a seemingly random pattern of lines and blocks, and as your eyes relaxed, you saw the picture hidden within.

That was the idea anyway, but Rob was buggered if he could ever get the damn thing to work. Maybe it was because he was born with a squint and had corrective eye surgery as a child, but whatever the reason, he could never see the magic picture.

George stocked a wide selection of Magic Eye books in the back, next to the *Viz* annuals and *Fangoria* magazines, and Rob's friends would invariably spend ages staring at them. "Oh, it's a cat!" one would shout. "Ahh, it's a rocket," another would pipe up, and all the time Rob would just be staring at a bunch of random squiggles.

Rob started to get jealous, really, really jealous. It was almost like his friends had another world that he wasn't privy to. It was like he was being shunned, excluded.

His friends had laughed at Rob's inability to discern the pictures. They had tried to help, after a fashion, but to no avail. They told him to let his eyes relax, easier said than done when you are staring, unblinking, at a jumble of blocks and lines.

Rob tried and tried and tried again. He tried all the various ridiculous methods suggested by his friends but none of them ever worked. The closest he came was when he tried after smoking dope, but in the end, he had become nauseated and forced to vomit. His friends thought that was hysterical.

****

One miserable Monday afternoon, Rob wandered through town despondently. He had skipped school early, which was usually a cause for celebration, but it was so he could go and have a rotting tooth yanked out, which was certainly not.

As he passed George's on his way home, a pang of envy hit him. He had managed to hustle a few quid at lunchtime by selling ciggies at an extortionate rate to desperate schoolmates, so he went inside.

Rob had enough loose change to purchase the cheapest Magic Eye book, a local, self-published affair by a local artist. It was touted to have been influenced by the works of Poe and *Hammer Horror* so it was right up Rob's street.

Once home, Rob locked his bedroom door, dimmed the lights, and set about conquering his adversary, the Magic Eye picture. He was determined to beat this thing; envy is a superb motivator.

Rob's eyes focused on the dingy red, black, and purple lines; he stared and stared. Nothing happened. Rob cursed and launched the book across the room.

After gathering his composure, he tried again. After what seemed like an eternity, something finally happened, but it wasn't what he expected. He expected to see Dracula's castle, or the raven perched above a chamber door, not a formless blob of questionable matter.

As he tried to make sense of the thing before his eyes, the form began to writhe and shift. Suddenly out of his peripheral vision, the room around him began to change. The light altered in hue, and the walls melted away. He would have altered his vision at that moment, but the mass held his gaze like a master hypnotist.

The cassette that played on his Hi-Fi faded away. It wasn't like deafness but more like it was smothered. Like when someone talks to you when you have your head under the bathwater. It was replaced by a throb, a pulse, almost a heartbeat…something alive.

The room had completely dissolved by now, replaced by the void—a swirling vista of emptiness. His blood roared in his ears, and his pulse raced. His breathing started to become forced and ragged.

Terror gripped Rob's heart like a vice as the form in the picture started to overflow the confines of the book. Tendrils of distorted colour and fronds of filthy-looking ichor started to wriggle hungrily towards him.

His stomach lurched like he was on a rollercoaster as a weightless feeling took firm hold of his body. He felt like he was drifting, untethered, and moments away from floating away into the deepest, darkest parts of the aether.

Rob's mind exploded with visions and whispers. The knowledge of things that no human should know began to subsume his feeling of self. Something was sucking the spirit, the will to live, out of his body with such ferocity that his lungs felt that they were about to burst.

The entity before his eyes surged and shuddered with hungry anticipation. It wanted Rob; it wanted his very existence. It had fully eclipsed the book and began to move, free of its anchor at last. With a surge and a piercing whistling sound, it lunged towards Rob.

The ghastly appendages strained and grasped for Rob, but he couldn't do anything to escape. He was glued to the spot, paralysed. The void rushed and tumbled around him as the roar of blood became deafening. Rob could feel his spirit, his very soul being sucked from his terror-slackened jaw. The form was inches from its feast when…

"Rob! How many times! Your dinner is ready!!"

Saved by a plate of fish fingers, oven chips, and baked beans, Rob hurled the book away from him in panic and managed to stutter, "Ok, Mum, down in a minute." He could hear her grumbling as she hobbled back downstairs. She probably thought he had been "discovering his body," Rob reflected ruefully.

Rob tried to fathom what had happened as he wolfed down the finest that Birds Eye, McCain, and Heinz had to offer, but drew a blank.

Later that evening, he took the book into the woods and burned it. He had no desire to repeat his experience. And as for his friends' private world, they could keep it. Rob was done with Magic Eye pictures.

The Elm of Dreams

by Clint Foster

In ancient times where magic resided, and myth and truth oft meet,

There was one who was known well among them, Reina, the elf maiden sweet.

Unbeknownst to Bol, the King, that young elf bent his realm,

And through her potent magic old, she summoned forth an elm.

The tree, you see, was not of Bol, a thing strange to Alkuran land,

But the magic which birthed it was not out of control, and its fate rested in Reina's hands.

She held this elm dear to her heart, for from her heart it sprung,

In the spring of the world and with love on her tongue. Upon its branches, her heart was hung.

From the ground, it sprouted proud and grew higher and higher still,

Watered by the fears of an elf-maiden's tears and born from her strength of will.

From all around came elves, so proud to kneel before Reina's tree,

For it bore a fruit of its magic roots that could fulfil both wishes and dreams.

But the tree did not give its gifts to all, and those whom it failed found,

Their souls were judged, and their hopes crushed, for in them evil was found.

More and more eova flocked to pray to the Elm of Dreams,

But even the best-intended gestures may be twisted to become evil deeds.

Those scorned by the elm and her magic fruit sought to steal its treasure.

The Vulkha, the Veiled ones, whose folly was in search of pleasure.

These elves had seen wishes fulfilled and dreams made reality.

Those who were denied could not help but

find themselves near green with envy.

Plots and schemes to steal wishes and dreams bore fruit of evil intent.

To the Elm of Dreams, for Reina to see, they, as an angry mob, went.

Demands and commands they spewed at her as she watered the tree with her tears.

These Vulkha she knew would come, too soon, to realise all her fears.

Their voices were boisterous as they boasted of justice, taking what was not theirs to take,

While Reina behind them cried, tried to stop them, for the tree's sake.

As they approached, they failed to note the tree was judging them anew,

Creating a sentence that each so deserved and granted their wishes askew.

Those Vulkha cruel, those wicked fools, they reached and with fingers pried.

One by one they ate the fruit. To them one by one it lied.

The first had dreamt of magic might to dominate his foes.

With sudden heat and searing meat, he

wished to overthrow.

A sorcerer, a conqueror, an emperor, a throne.

Power without measure, a potent treasure, that he wished to have all alone.

The next wished wisdom would win over wars but wished to be wisest of all.

He desired the power to see every past, future, rise, and fall.

None could know for certain the future, none could know the past,

Unless he deigned to answer them the questions which they asked.

Another, a dream for all to be unbroken, hard as stone.

This one vied for a protection denied, for he wished to be safe alone.

Defending who he wished to keep alive, for his chosen price.

He alone would decide each battle who lives and who soon dies.

Another for water, and ships, and honour to travel on swift golden wings.

To discover other people and worlds. To be

to them gods and kings.

The last for blood, for war and drums, and in the end for him to be left.

When all others were slain, he alone would remain, and war, on his shoulders, he'd heft.

At the end of all battles, he wished to saddle death itself and rule.

Just as once young Tykus had done. His was a wish for fools.

So they ate, and sat, and waited, and those thieves together then thought,

The tales of the elm indeed were true, and to all of them, their gifts, it brought.

Not the way they hoped and prayed, for their hearts and souls were stained,

And the Elm of Dreams did not foresee any reason to soothe their pain.

Power wished for granted in full, but now entrapped within.

The first the Totem of Lightning became, and many battles he would win.

Prophecy and the gift to see were offered to the second thief,

Then he was trapped in a rock with no voice

to talk. His totem brings only grief.

To the third was given perhaps the closest sentence to his wishes dear,

Then he, the Totem of Stone, was buried alone. The first to reappear.

The next into the river Nazene was suck and buried deep.

Never again to be found in the ground beneath those currents that sweep.

For the last, the one who craved the glory that comes with vict'ry in arms,

He found a fate not good, but great, and his wish caused terrible harm.

For the Totem, you see, the stone that was he, gave power beyond all measure.

It was hidden away until later days, when was found the ultimate treasure.

When Reina could rise, she saw and cried at the fates of the Vulkha, the fools,

Who sought to use her magic for ill and used the wishing fruit as a tool.

"When I sang to the trees of magic and dreams, those trees sang back to me.

When I wished for a world where wishes are

heard, of a future for all to see.

The Elm of Dreams grew for me and you, and the good whose intent is just.

It bears a fruit off mystical shoots, and they ne'er rot nor fall to the dust.

Her silver leaves and golden sleeves dazzle with auric lustre,

Try though they did, the wicked, insidious Vulkha proved only bluster.

For those evil elves came, the ones whose names are cursed to be burned from the lists.

They wished for power and more, then war, and the world around them to shift.

So the Elm of Dreams granted their wishes each, though not in the way they foresaw.

For that magic which grew so strong, and through it the Vulkha were judged for their flaw.

They ate the fruit from the silver shoots, and they drank of the golden sap.

They kept all others from treating with the tree, and all its power they hoped to tap.

Perhaps they succeeded for they got what they dreamed of, but the Elm of Dreams took revenge.

For it made of them stones, totems of bones, and itself, the tree avenged.

As the gleam and the sheen left the tree of the queen, I saw a flash fit to blind Bol.

So bright that light that shone did seem, it burned the Vulkha's souls.

With a blink they were gone, to what world beyond awaits those who don't achieve Godhall,

And when that moment was done, the tree had won, for though dulled, it did not fall.

At its trunk then lay those stones through which the old magic now grows. Through the Totems of the Vulkha's souls, the most sought-after power flows.

By their wish, now granted, a new magic tree planted, with a seed that fell and was caught,

To be nurtured and loved, and watered and sung to, and kept neither too cold nor too hot.

As I shall tend it I hope someday to mend it and go back to the wood where it lives.

For once it is grown, I hope it will show there is more for my magic to give."

So Reina's tree and its magic seed had foiled the Vulkha's plan.

And without so meaning they ended up weaning old magic away from the land.

Heaven

by Kelly Matsuura

Symal had visited Heaven recently for a conference. He hadn't cared for the people—those do-gooders who never stop smiling and wishing you well. But the rest of it was a demon's dream!

The organic sheets in the hotel? Sweet indulgence. Hand-rolled cigars and endless cocktails in the bar? Divine. And the food! *Everything* was on offer. His favourite was a huge, pickled cow's head, accompanied with honey-smoked giraffe's testicles. Pure wickedness.

His friends were envious. When one got too mouthy though, he stuffed his last premium cigar down that loser's throat.

"What?" he asked the witnesses. "Heaven isn't rehab."

The Sin

by David Green

Allvar sat cross-legged in the meadow, his back to the magnificent oak tree that dominated the skyline for miles around. He tilted his face, so the sun's gentle rays caressed it. The beauty of birds singing played in his ears. In the distance, Allvar could see a stone tower reaching into the heavens, a single window and balcony facing his way. His home these last three hundred years. Memories of his time before coming to the meadow had faded, as had his purpose for seeking it out. Allvar's life before finding his new path was over; all that mattered was what his future held.

Breathing a contented sigh, Allvar closed his eyes and rested his head against the bark.

"Why do we come here?" came a voice from behind the tree.

Allvar turned, having forgotten about his

companion. Wulf sat with his knees drawn up, head in hands, his white robe dirty and creased. Allvar glanced down at his own. *Pristine, as it should be,* he thought with a satisfied smile.

"We come to meditate on what our Master has taught us," Allvar chided, "you know that."

They arrived into the meadow together, all those years before. They hadn't looked alike then, but Allvar could see they'd grown to resemble each other since. Their eye colour had changed to a bright green, their hair and beards snowy. By their faces, they looked to be men of middle years, but their stares held their age.

"I can't concentrate," Wulf complained with bitterness. "It's like I can't grasp His lessons anymore."

"Why don't you go home and rest?" Allvar replied, nodding to a tower identical to his own in the distance that belonged to Wulf. Neither men built them, the keeps had been there long before their arrival.

"I think I will," Wulf said, struggling to his feet with weariness. "It's all right for you, Allvar. You understand what He tells us before He's even said it sometimes. I don't know what I'm doing here."

The man slumped away, head bowed, oblivious to the beauty of the afternoon. Allvar shook his head with a rueful smile on his face. Not that he tried to be better than his companion, it seemed natural. He closed his eyes again and emptied his mind, allowing the sounds of the meadow to wash over him.

You should guide Wulf, my son. His confidence is low, but his soul believes in my purpose.

"Master," Allvar replied out loud to the voice of his God that whispered in his head. "I've tried to tell him, but he won't listen to me."

Perhaps you should attend instead of instructing, Allvar. A humble man explains through actions, not words. Be wary of prideful thoughts, they can become envious soon enough.

Allvar opened his eyes, hoping to glimpse his Master. The tree stood where he and Wulf first came across Him. He would appear from time to time but would often communicate directly to their minds. Their Master prepared them to leave the meadow. When that time would be, and their purpose, Allvar and Wulf didn't know.

Finding himself alone, Allvar scoffed. *Some are too stupid to learn. If only my Master could understand that.*

His mood soured, Allvar left the tree and walked towards his tower, wondering if his time to leave this place grew near. On the horizon, he could see dark clouds gathering. They never seemed to move into the meadow but, of late, their darkness grew more prominent.

***

"What do you remember before you came here?"

The words whispered from every corner of the dark room Allvar stood in. He couldn't recall getting to this place, or where it was. The room's only light came from a dying fire. Four bare, wooden walls surrounded him with no windows or doors he could see.

"I have no memory of my life before the meadow," Allvar shouted, glancing around with a wild stare. Feeling his skin erupt into goose bumps, he realised he stood naked. A thick layer of grime covered every part of his visible skin. "Where am I? Who are you?"

"Fan the flames and see."

Allvar crouched and approached the dying fire. Some lessons his Master taught were in using will. It seemed like magic when his instruction began. Now he knew his resolve to be strong enough to have some control over the world. Allvar thrust a finger at the embers.

"Fire," he muttered.

The flames ignored him. Allvar frowned.

"Fire!" he roared.

A laugh echoed around him.

"Try the stones. Or have you forgotten how to do things with your hands? You used to be good at that."

Scowling, Allvar grabbed two rocks from beside the pit and began striking them against the other. He lost himself in the rhythm. Without the disembodied voice, silence hung in the air. It took him a while, but he realised not even the stones made a sound. Allvar gasped in disbelief and fell backwards as a single spark fell into the flames, turning the fire into a conflagration.

Throwing an arm across his face, Allvar scrambled back, fearful of what he'd created.

"Look beyond the fire."

Strange, he thought, *the voice sounds like mine when I mock Wulf.* Allvar lowered his arm, his eyes wide as he discovered the flames under control, though he felt no heat from them. An orange glow illuminated the room. On the other side of the fire lay a body. Its naked and dirty back to Allvar.

He crept forward on all fours, stopping a yard away. The body didn't move, not even from the slow rise of breath leaving and entering its lungs. Allvar reached out with a tentative arm and grabbed the shoulder, turning the body towards him.

No, he thought as he peered at the face, his hand covering his slack jaw in shock. *It can't be.*

Allvar looked closer at the dead man. The hair on his head and beard wasn't the colour of snow, but the man was Allvar's doppelganger.

"How…" Allvar began, only to break off as

the dead man's eyelids shot open, his face twisting in rage.

With a snarl, the doppelganger leapt at Allvar, knocking him to the floor then reaching for his neck and choking him. Allvar beat at the man's ribs, chest, and head but he didn't let go. The grip became stronger the more Allvar struggled.

Life left his limbs, and he fought for air, his vision growing dim. Allvar stared up into his twin's face, seeing hate and fury reflected.

Just as Allvar thought he was about to breathe his last, the pressure was released. His body lurched, and he fell to the ground with a thud.

Twisting around on the floor, Allvar found himself alone in his tower bedroom, his bedclothes twisted around his neck. Panting, he crawled to the balcony and looked out across the meadow. A light shone in the opposite tower's window. Lightning crackled on the horizon.

***

You seem distracted.

Allvar's eyes flew open, feeling his Master's words directed at him and not Wulf. Seated at the foot of the colossal tree in the meadow, the day was a rare occasion where their Master joined them. Allvar didn't know if He was physically there, as the being's body seemed to be more light than flesh. Allvar looked away and narrowed his eyes at Wulf, sitting opposite him. The man's face serene as he meditated.

"Sorry, Master," Allvar muttered. "Ill thoughts invaded my dreams, and I am not myself. I'm surprised you're full of life, Wulf. Unless you've taken to sleeping with your candle lit."

The other man's eyes blinked open, and he looked sidelong at his Master, cheeks flushing.

"I studied my thoughts late into the night," he replied, "though I feel refreshed."

"Night air will do that, I'm sure," Allvar snapped.

"What do you mean, Allvar?"

"You know ex…"

Enough. A whisper from their Master

silenced the men's tongues. Allvar glared down at the grass.

Tell me, my sons. Are all men equal?

"Yes, we're all created the same," Allvar replied without thinking. He closed his eyes and bit down on his tongue when he realised his mistake. His Master would not permit a second attempt at an answer.

"Master?" Wulf spoke into the silence. "I don't agree. We're created the same, but don't our actions dictate our worth?"

Allvar scowled as he felt his Master's approval wash over the other man.

Wulf, do you believe a man trapped by their past actions?

Allvar continued to bite on his tongue, feeling the sharp tang of iron filling his mouth. *He attacked me last night. I'm sure of it. Jealous that I'm the better student. Now he tries to take my place.*

"I think actions can't be forgotten, Master," Wulf replied, smiling. "But if a man shows penance and desire to learn and grow, we should encourage him and lend support."

Very good, my son. That will be all for today. Allvar, please rest. I sense a change in you.

As his Master drifted away into the sunlight, Allvar shot to his feet and loomed over Wulf. The other man stood, and they faced each other, noses almost touching.

"I know what you did to me," Allvar snarled. "Or tried to do. Why?"

Wulf laughed in a more high-pitched way than normal. "Our Master is right," he replied, taking a step back. "You need some rest."

"How dare you!" Allvar shouted, raising his fist. Neither man could use his will on the other, by their Master's design.

"This is not like you," Wulf said, jumping backwards. "You've not acted in anger for almost three hundred years!"

"You are beneath me," Allvar roared, shaking his fist. "Now you try to take my place? You? The village idiot. Begone before I strike you down."

Wulf nodded to himself, his face sad. With a shake of his head, he turned and walked towards his own tower.

Allvar spat on the ground, then took a step backward. He crouched and looked behind him. The grass where the two men stood had turned black.

***

For Allvar, the nights and days blended into one. Nightmares followed more bickering with Wulf. In his dreams, sometimes he killed, and just as often, he murdered. Some nights, the dreams felt more like memories or visions than make believe.

Their Master stayed away, but, by the look on Wulf's face as they sat beneath the tree, Allvar could see they spoke in his mind. The clouds on the horizon darkened and grew in size. Exhausted, Allvar longed to escape the meadow.

After a bitter disagreement with Wulf, Allvar stomped back to his tower and stewed on his balcony, watching the other man's tower in case he saw him approach. During the night, Allvar passed out in his chair.

"You've always considered me lesser."

Allvar lurched forward as the voice woke him but found he couldn't move from his chair. Wulf sat opposite him on the balcony, a sad smile on his face.

"I often wonder at how alike our faces have become," Wulf said, leaning forward and tracing a finger down Allvar's nose.

"How are you doing this?" Allvar stammered, straining to move.

"I'm not restraining you, my old friend," Wulf replied. "I'm commanding the surrounding air instead. Strange you've never figured this out yourself."

"Are you planning on killing me?"

Wulf laughed, though a tear ran down his cheek.

"I've wanted nothing more than for you to respect me. When I realised that could never be, I desired only friendship and guidance. Why could you never give me that?"

Allvar stayed silent as he watched the other man carefully, and with more than a small amount of fear.

Wulf stood and crouched in front of Allvar,

eyes meeting.

"I loved you like a brother, Allvar," he whispered. "Something has changed in me. I understand our purpose."

Allvar flinched as Wulf moved forward, expecting the worse. Instead, the other man kissed him on the forehead and left the tower without a backwards glance. Allvar remained seated as he watched Wulf journey across the meadow. Howling with hot anger and regret, and free of the restraints Wulf had laid on him, Allvar threw his chair over the balcony's edge. He sank to his knees and wept, dismayed that Wulf had bested him in a way Allvar never could.

***

Allvar arrived at the meadow's mighty tree to find his Master and Wulf waiting for him. He sensed disapproval from his Master hitting him in waves. He'd looked in a mirror before he left. Sunken eyes stared back, his hair wild and dishevelled. Allvar slowed his step as he approached the pair, stopping a small distance away.

Sit, Allvar.

"I'll stand, Master."

As you please, his Master replied, turning towards Wulf and motioning him forward. *The time has come to send you back into the world. To spread what I have taught. I had hoped to send you both. Wulf will go alone.*

Rage boiled up inside Allvar; he felt his face twist without his permission. His bones seemed to bend as he hunched, though he knew that to be his imagination. He glowered up at the other man from beneath his brows.

"Congratulations, Wulf," he muttered with a shrug. "Is that all, Master?"

It is for your own well-being, Allvar. You need more time with me, alone. You are returning to how you were before. Wulf has always been humbler than you. That fault is mine.

"As you say, Master," Allvar said. With a last look at Wulf, he turned and returned to his tower.

***

A quick learner, Allvar had spent the rest of the day practising what Wulf had executed on him. He'd practised until he could suspend objects in the air. Now, after darkness had fallen, he sat on the edge of Wulf's bed as the other man slept, confident his will would hold him in place.

"Wake up," Allvar commanded.

Wulf's eyes blinked open then grew wider as he saw he wasn't alone. Colour drained from his face when he realised he couldn't move.

"Allvar," he began, "I didn't mean to make you envious of me. I tried to make you and our Master proud."

Allvar laughed as he gazed around the room. Exerting his will, six sharpened pieces of wood drifted to the bed, each the length of his forearm. There were no weapons in the meadow, but Allvar had taken branches from the tree they'd sat at every day and fashioned stakes out of them.

"Do you remember the time before we came here?" he asked, holding one of the wooden nails and examining it. "I do. My dreams have taught me where the Master wouldn't. He's turned us into sheep. I used to take what I wanted when it suited me. He brought us here because He failed humanity, and we turned our back on Him. Now, He's failed again."

Allvar held the stake up high and drove it through the palm of Wulf's hand, straight through it and into the mattress and bedframe beneath. Blood leaked from the wound as Wulf cried out in shock and pain. Thunder rumbled in the distance.

"Why are you doing this?" Wulf sobbed, the bedsheets on one side turning crimson.

"Because you tried to kill me. Strangling me in my sleep like a coward!" Allvar replied, plunging a second shaft through Wulf's other hand, smiling at his screams.

"I didn't," Wulf shouted through his cries. "Please!"

"Liar," Allvar whispered, though he suspected Wulf told the truth.

"He meant us to save the world outside," Wulf screamed as Allvar drove a stake through his ankle, laughing through delirium. "They need our guidance."

The thunder grew louder. Allvar tapped one of his weapons against his lip as he gazed down at the blood pooling on the bed, dripping onto the floor. He remembered enjoying killing, three hundred years ago, before he wandered into the meadow, seeking refuge from people who chased him for murder. Before his Master had tried to change him. *To prove his point,* Allvar thought, *I've proved him wrong. Men don't change.*

"What has the world outside ever done for me?" he asked, before nailing Wulf's last limb to the mattress, smiling as the wood drove through Wulf's ligaments and bone.

"Two stakes left..." Allvar muttered, climbing on top of the stricken man, not caring that he knelt in the blood leaking from him.

"You're killing me because you're jealous of me," Wulf whispered, too weak to put more effort in his voice. Tears slid from his eyes, which held pain and pity. The look made Allvar rage inside, all the more because Wulf spoke the truth.

"I'm killing you because I can," Allvar whispered, dropping the stakes and putting his hands around Wulf's throat. "Look at me until the light disappears."

Allvar squeezed as he choked the life from his

old friend's body and continued to grasp him long after Wulf had died. Letting go, he stared at the dead man.

"We looked so alike, didn't we?" he said as he picked up the last two stakes and plunged them through Wulf's eyes, pinning his head to the pillow.

Allvar staggered to his feet and descended the tower without looking back, his feet taking him to the tree. He looked up when he approached, seeing the storm on the horizon rage against the invisible barrier that held it at bay.

Examining the mighty oak, Allvar drew on all the will he could muster and threw his arms towards it.

"Fire!"

Flames engulfed the tree, the snapping of wood filling Allvar's ears. Turning away from the towers, he strode away into the world outside as the storm broke through. Allvar felt rain on his face for the first time in three hundred years, though he knew no amount of water could wash away the blood he'd spilled and the sin he carried with him beyond the meadow.

Forever Home

by T.M. Brown

The turn-of-the-century Craftsman across from Clark residence was perfect. Its porch was spacious and breezy. Verdant baskets of ferns and purple petunias hung from its overhanging eaves. The old, twin oaks in the front yard were positioned in a manner that was neither too symmetrical nor too unruly. Its thick, tapered columns were the epitome of the architectural style. Of course, the old home had a lovely history to it as well. Not only had it been home to local luminary Clive Rockwell, but it had once been the residence of her Great Aunt Cornelia Stephenson, a prominent local civil rights activist. The house was just…perfect.

For nearly a decade, Amy Clark had watched as the Miller family squatted in the residence that by all rights should have been hers. She watched from across the street as they ate dinner together, as the two children played with their dog, as John took out the trash… She followed the heartbeat of their marriage like it was her own little reality show. With her children off to college and her husband often away on business, Amy increasingly found herself with little else to do. What had started as curiosity became jealousy and, eventually, obsession.

Amy kept real estate apps up on her phone at all times, waiting patiently for the day when the Millers decided to move. Years and hundreds of thousands of refreshes later, they were still there—watering their perfect lawn and lounging about on their perfect porch. Eventually, Amy determined she could not leave such matters to fate. She began timing her walks to coincide with Julia's early morning jogs. She would bring up any issue that she thought might entice them to move—house prices were up, local crime was increasing, the schools were in decline. Nothing worked. She'd tried to be subtle at first but as time wore on, Amy became increasingly persistent and direct. Her relationship with the Millers became strained.

After her more direct attempts to influence the squatters failed, Amy had taken to trying to induce them to leave via social media. Under a variety of different accounts, she left awful reviews for every business and service she could think of—restaurants, shops, schools, libraries— she targeted them all. Not even playgrounds escaped her campaign of scathing reviews. When that produced no results, she took to bullying the youngest Miller through fake accounts. Children really could be so cruel. Amy noticed considerable changes in the kid's behaviour, but her parents still refused to move.

Her husband, Gerald, became increasingly concerned about her. He had suggested that they simply relocate to another neighbourhood. His opinion scarcely mattered, however. He was rarely around anyway. She belonged on that shaded porch beneath the purple petunias. That Craftsman was *her* house.

On a sunny summer afternoon, she walked right up the winding granite stairs to the Miller residence and knocked on the front door. When Devin opened the door, she could see past him into the living room. The decor was a bit tasteless, but the layout was just lovely. She'd offered right then to pay whatever it took to buy the home. She could afford it. Gerald made more in four months than the Millers made in an entire year. Both Devin and Julia worked for the city. Their income was a matter of public record.

The moment they turned her down, everything finally made sense. She stood on the porch and took in her surroundings. She could smell the petunias and the freshly cut grass. Despite being a warm, summer day, the shaded porch felt pleasantly cool. The airflow there was just ideal. She understood that the Millers would never leave her home. Why would they? It was just too perfect. She smiled, thanked them for their time, and returned across the street.

After the grisly murders in the turn-of-the-century Craftsman, Gerald and Amy Clark were able to purchase it for a steal. Amy repeatedly flipped through pictures of the house on her phone as they drove to the bank to close on their new home. It was just so lovely now that the blood stains had been removed. Traffic was backed up on the interstate, and Gerald had taken them through a residential area on the north side of the city. The car came to a stop at a shady intersection.

"Hey, darling. Take a look at that Victorian," Gerald commented. "It's really nice." Amy looked up from her phone. It was *really* nice. The canopy of the mature trees surrounding it shimmied in the soft breeze. The house's steeply pitched roof and textured shingles were the very epitome of the architectural style. As the car pulled through the quiet intersection, Amy couldn't help but wonder who lived there.

Anything You Can Do

by Lyndsey Ellis-Holloway

Magic crackled in the air. Its unmistakable metallic taste left a slight tingle on top of his tongue like an electric shock.

An elderly lady struggled with her shopping bags and the door to the apartment block. Adriel jogged over and took the bags from her with a smile. She held the door for him, negating the magic intended to keep people like himself out.

He carried her bags full of groceries under one arm; milk, eggs, and a variety of other food items cradled against his side as they entered the elevator, chatting away as they made their way to the third floor.

"Where do you want me to put the bags, Rose?" he asked as he manoeuvred past her through the door.

"Just on the kitchen counter would be lovely. Do you want a cup of tea? It's the least I can do."

"Thank you but no, I have to get off. I have a surprise for my brother, and I have to get it done before he gets home." Adriel smiled, waving as he made his way back to the elevator.

"See you soon!" Rose called after him, and Adriel chuckled under his breath. She had no idea how true that statement was.

Adriel stepped out of the elevator as he reached the fourth floor, striding down the corridor with purpose, glancing over his shoulder as though he expected to find his brother hiding round the corner. It was paranoia—he knew it was—but the detour with Rose had taken time, and he didn't have much to play with.

Standing in front of the door, he held his hand out, palm millimetres from the surface, his fingers spread wide. The warding crackled and struck out, warning him against touching it. His brow furrowed, and he took a step back, knocking an abandoned beer bottle with his foot. It clattered against the door behind him.

The corridor was filled with loud barking,

and Adriel hissed under his breath, looking up and down the corridor, as a couple of voices cursed "that damned dog" or yelled for it to "shut the hell up," but thankfully no one left their homes. Adriel held his breath and looked back at the elevator doors, exhaling as they remained firmly shut.

He glanced back at the bottle he had kicked and smiled. Adriel picked up the empty bottle, filling it with some of his own magic, just enough to trick the warding in the door, and threw the bottle at it. The bottle struck the door, and a bolt of gold lightning eviscerated the bottle into glittering dust.

The warding wouldn't harm a human being; his brother had no need to ward himself against *them*. The magic was familiar, but it was older than anything he had encountered before. It was similar in reaction to the warding used by the ancient Greeks, but the golden hue was far more like...of course, what else? Adriel snorted, closing his eyes and gathering his power into his hands as he whispered in a language unrecognisable to anyone other than his family, though even some of the younger siblings would not know it.

Placing his hands against the door before turning the knob, he heard the lock click. He smiled, glancing at the elevator doors again as though he expected to see Sammael standing there looking at him. He had to be quick.

Ancient Enochian warding spells, what *else* would his brother use? And he was supposed to be the *clever* one. For all his brother's bravado and knowledge of the world (he had centuries over Adriel, so *technically* he had more experience), he remained predictable.

The air inside the apartment was cloying and heavy with the smell of stale cigarette smoke. *This* was what his brother had given everything up for? *This?* This *hovel*. Ensuring the door was closed, he moved into the living room, looking around in disdain, lip curled at the state of the place.

This whole room *stank* of stale cigarettes, with every breath Adriel could feel it clawing at his throat—was it any wonder Sammael drank whiskey when you had to contend with the air in this room? The blame for *that* particular habit fell upon the Aztecs since they had invented cigarettes, but it did not matter; it was still beyond foul and certainly not becoming of an Angel.

Adriel ran his fingers along the edge of the sideboard, nose wrinkling in disgust as the dust gathered beneath his fingertips.

Flicking the dust from his fingers, he cast his gaze over the one-bedroom apartment. One old two-seater sofa—Adriel couldn't even hazard a guess at the colour it had been when it was new— the grotty, faded grey-green didn't look particularly inviting. The television opposite the sofa was cumbersome, and a layer of dust covered the remote on top of the set. The bed, while fully made, was covered with moth-bitten sheets, wrinkled from being sat on. But like everything else in this apartment, there was a layer of filth on its surface.

This was a place for his brother to keep his belongings rather than a place of sanctuary or pleasure. Adriel allowed his head to roll onto his shoulder, glancing at the sideboard and the trails his fingers left upon the wooden surface.

Something deep down told him he should be worried about his brother spotting the break in the dust, but he wasn't remotely concerned. In fact, he *wanted* his sibling to spot it, then his brother would realise that he wasn't as clever or all-powerful as he seemed to believe.

Why did the others fear him? Look at the absolute mess he had become! He was as far from the man they had known as possible. At home he had been a beacon, a shining example of God's brilliance personified, and his work had been impeccable until their Father had allowed him to indulge in a family.

Now? Now he was a slob who indulged in drinking at every opportunity and smoked like the Gates of Hell. He was pathetic; he was Fallen. Yet *still*, the others worried that Sammael would come home, or that he would somehow cause dissent amongst their family from this putrid pigsty.

Adriel had watched his brother and learned from him lest he was required to take up Sammael's mantle for whatever reason. That was the purpose he was given upon his Creation Day, and he had been elated—Sammael was the best of them as far as Adriel had been concerned, and it was clear to anyone with eyes that Sammael was Father's favourite.

Sammael had broken their Father's heart, also Adriel's, when he had chosen to Fall. Despite the heartache, Adriel had stepped into his role under the suffocating shadow his brother left in his wake.

Adriel caught sight of his reflection out of the corner of his eye and turned to look at himself in the greasy, cockeyed mirror. Where Sammael had been recognised and admired, Adriel went unnoticed, even in a position of power such as his. He was overlooked by *all* the Host. He deserved better; he deserved their admiration just as much—no, *more* so—than his brother! He would never dream of straying from the path their Father had given to him, but he knew that none of his family had actually expected him to take on the title; they had believed he would be wait in the shadow of his brother's brilliance for all eternity.

"I worshipped you, brother," he snarled. "You never even looked at me, but I *still* idolised you, and *this* is how you live now? You chose *this* over us? I don't know whether I should be more disgusted with you or myself for wanting to *be* like you."

He was the end of everything, not Sammael, not anymore, so why did they not see him! Despite Sammael's betrayal, their Father *still* pined for His son's return.

"*I* am *Death*!" Adriel lashed out, slamming his fist into the mirror so hard that it slid from its weak moorings and smashed into the floor. Shards of glass scattered across the threadbare carpet. Well, there would be no hiding that someone had been here now; let that be a lesson to his brother that he was weaker than he thought.

The other gods, the Pagans and Egyptians, the Greeks and the rest—those heathens barely looked his way when he came to collect their dead; while he continued to do his duty as was his right, they sneered and commented about he was not half the man Sammael had been.

"Oi! Keep it down in there!" The voice was muffled through the walls and he snorted, his brother's neighbour was lucky that Adriel had other priorities; otherwise, the man might have found himself in an early grave. Adriel shook his head as he felt the suppressive force of his siblings speaking to one another from Heaven.

Even now the Host spoke their Fallen brother's name in hushed, awestruck tones, recounting the tales of his work to one another as though he were still within their ranks. Yes, there was hatred and disappointment amongst the voices, but at least they did not dismiss Sammael as they did Adriel. No one spoke of him with such reverence. In fact, most days Adriel wondered whether the majority of his siblings knew he even existed.

They would.

Soon.

Adriel smiled at himself in the broken shards. Everything he was working on was so they would finally see *him*. Once he completed his work, Father would *have* to recognise him— at long last Father would see Adriel for who he was and realise the potential in the son He had placed in Sammael's shadow all those centuries ago.

The Archangel picked up the decanter of whiskey from the sideboard, turning the heavy, carved crystal around upon his fingertips as he watched the caramel-coloured liquid within slosh about. His brother had picked up some terrible habits in his time: a consequence of being too close to the heathens; Sammael had always indulged the other gods even to the point of *marrying* into the Greeks.

Father had allowed His son to get away with far too much, and Sammael's union to Morta had been doomed from the outset. No one looked at him that way; no man, woman, nor beast looked longingly at Adriel, most looked through him it seemed. Sammael had married—he'd had a *daughter*. Yes, he'd lost her, but he at least had a child of his own. What did Adriel have?

As much as he despised Sammael for abandoning his post, as much as he wanted the recognition for the work he did, Adriel had admired his brother for being able to complete his duty (once upon a time) and still have a life of his own.

Setting the decanter back into its place, he

caught sight of a reflection on its surface, Adriel turned away from it and glanced back towards the door as though he expected to find Sammael standing there already. All thoughts of being caught vanished when he spotted what he had come for. It was nothing fancy—there was no elaborate decoration to the hilt; to those who didn't know any better, it was just a plain sword. The blade positively gleamed despite the dingy lighting. To Adriel, it was a thing of beauty.

Anger surged within him, the loathing and frustration causing his body to tense.

Scythe.

His brother's sword.

No. That was not right.

Death's sword.

By rights, the blade belonged to *him*. Yet another thing Sammael had kept hold of despite his fall from grace. Well, no longer, the other slights Adriel would remedy in time, but this one he would rectify *now*.

The hairs on the back of his neck stood to attention as a shiver ran down his spine, his nerves on fire, prickled against his skin. Sammael had returned: it was time to leave and take what belonged to him.

Adriel grasped Scythe by the hilt. His knuckles froze in place as an intense heat and glow emanated from the glowing sword. His arm trembled, jaw aching as he gritted his teeth against the pain roaring through his body. His head whipped towards the door at the sound of a key in the lock, and he threw himself towards the window. With his free hand, Adriel undid the lock and pushed the window open, launching himself out, flicking his wings, and returning to the Heavens, just as Sammael opened the door to his apartment.

Too close.

***

Arriving outside the walls to the Golden City, Adriel collapsed to the ground and screamed; his free hand gripped the wrist of the hand still attached to Scythe, attempting to support it. His entire hand felt like it was on fire. The metal was so hot that his hand had gone cold, his entire body trembling as pain reverberated through him. Was the sword refusing him? Nc! It was his *right*, he was Death now and Scythe belonged to *him*. It was not fair that it rejected him as it did—Sammael was no longer its Master!

The smell of charred flesh filled his nostrils, and Adriel bit back a wave of nausea. He shifted his weight, manoeuvring himself so he could plant one foot atop the blade and pull his arm away from the sword as he used his good hand to peel his fingers away. His teeth clamped together as he was forced to tear his flesh down to the bone to relinquish the blade.

Finally, Scythe allowed its thief to free himself. Adriel fell backwards, clutching his injured hand to his chest.

He bared his teeth as he moved his arm enough to look at the wound; his fingers still curled inward as though the hilt remained in his grasp. The flesh was charred and red. Raw, white blisters formed around his palm, exposing patches of bone around his bloodied, mangled fingers.

He would have to speak to Raphael and get

her to heal it. He doubted she would ask any questions, yet another example of how little his siblings thought of him despite who he was. Snarling, he stood up, looming over the sword.

"*I* am your Master now, regardless of what you think. I am Adriel, Angel of Death, you belong to *me*," he sneered, ripping a strip of cloth from his robes to wind around his hand, before using it to pick up the blade. He could feel it revolt, could feel the heat as it intensified, but the damage was already done, and he would not allow it to beat him again.

It belonged to him, whether it liked it or not. It was merely the first step in getting what was rightfully his. Injured hand clutched to his chest, he spread his pure white wings, flexing the powerful muscles, and grimaced against the pain. They would see. All of them. They would see.

 The Wingman

by V.A. Vazquez

Becca lit the final candle from the 99-cent box she'd purchased at Dollar General. The flame flickered for a moment before settling on top of the wick, and she edged it into the circle she'd assembled on her bedroom carpet. She'd printed out an incantation from Reddit.

"O Mighty Satan," she said, "I grant thee the power to manifest in my mind. Give me a true and faithful answer, so that I may accomplish my desired ends. This I humbly ask in Your Name, Lord Satan, may you deem me worthy."

Her gerbil scuttled about in its cardboard box, scratching at the walls with its pushpin claws. *Scritch-scritch-scritch.* She let it scoot into the palm of her hand. "Sorry, Mr Neepers." She plopped him down onto her toolbox altar and raised a paperweight high above her head. "If it's any consolation, gerbils are only supposed to live for three years. You didn't have much time left, anyway."

And with that, she brought the paperweight down hard on Mr Neepers' head. He gave a high-pitched *squeak* before he expired, his blood and brain matter seeping out like raspberry jam. As soon as her blood sacrifice had been smeared across the altar, a wind whipped around her bedroom, extinguishing all the candles.

Becca sat there in silence, too terrified to twitch a muscle. What would happen now? Would her floor crack open and hellfire ignite her curtains? Would Satan himself emerge from the shadows, his hoofed feet clomping across the carpet? Would she be immolated and condemned to damnation for her sacrilege?

Hey.

She let out a squeak to rival Mr Neepers' and scrambled under the bed, hiding from whatever had just appeared in her bedroom.

What can I do for you?

She peered out from beneath the dust ruffle, but no one was there.

That's because I'm inside your mind. The place you wanted me to go, remember?

"Satan?" Becca whispered.

Yes?

"It really worked? I'm possessed by Satan?"

Ask and ye shall receive.

Becca popped out from under the bed. "O Mighty Satan, I have summoned you here to help me fulfil my desires."

And those are…?

"Well, there's this boy—"

Fuck. I'm out.

"No!" She grabbed the remains of Mr Neepers and thrust him towards the ceiling, his caved-in head falling limply to one side. "I murdered my gerbil for you. At least listen to my problem."

A sigh echoed against the bone walls of her skull.

Fine. For Mr Neepers.

"I have always been a good church-going girl. I lead the weekly prayer meetings at the CYO centre and make all the placards for our abortion clinic protests and play acoustic guitar at sermon every Sunday."

Wow.

"And during one of those sermons, I saw *him* in the front row."

And who exactly is he?

"Father Peña."

...Go on.

She dropped Mr Neepers back onto the altar and sat down, crossed-legged, on her bedroom floor.

"He's the most handsome man I've ever seen," she said. "He's got eyes the same colour as those little Dove Chocolates with the inspirational messages printed on the wrappers. Every time I look at him, my heart ignites with a flame brighter than the Holy Spirit."

You do know you summoned Satan into your bedroom, right?

"Sure. Why?"

Because you don't sound like my usual clientele.

"I wouldn't normally call on the Son of Perdition to help me out with anything," she said. "But there's a small problem."

What is it?

"Father Peña's the chief exorcist for the Archdiocese of Rhode Island."

Satan remained silent.

"It's the only way I can get his attention!" Becca tossed Mr Neepers into the trash can and started stacking the candles back into their box. "I've tried everything else. I was even on the planning committee for the Annual Diocesan Youth Day because I was *sure* he'd be there. But my friend, Matthew? He's an altar server. He says there's been an uptick in exorcism requests, and Father Peña's busy with all those demonic possessions."

So you decided to get possessed by Satan.

"Uh-huh," she said. "So will you help me?"

…I think we might be able to work something out.

***

When Father Peña arrived the following afternoon, Becca had already been tied to the bedframe by her parents. Her hair was greasier than the BP oil spill in the Gulf of Mexico; her eyes were the colour of a urine sample.

"I can't believe he's going to see me like this," she said, looking at her reflection in the full-length mirror on her wall. "I probably smell like the YWCA locker room."

They listened as the priest climbed the staircase and pushed Becca's bedroom door open. She struggled against the nylon ropes her father had bought from Home Depot, while the priest set his satchel down in the corner and removed a bottle of Holy Water.

"We drive you from us," Father Peña read from a notebook, pushing his glasses up onto the bridge of his nose. "Whoever you may be: unclean spirits, all satanic powers, all infernal invaders…"

"It's just me again."

The words came out of Becca's mouth, even though she wasn't the one who'd spoken them.

"It's…oh, for Christ's sake." Father Peña slammed the door shut. "You can't keep doing this."

"Doing what?"

"Possessing college girls. It's a violation of their bodily autonomy."

"How else am I supposed to see you?"

"You're not *supposed* to see me. I'm a priest; you're…"

"Satan?"

Father Peña crossed his arms against his chest. And underneath that black button-down shirt and starched white collar, what a firm and toned chest it was.

Um, what's going on here? Do you two know each other?

Of course we do. You said it yourself. He's the chief exorcist for the Archdiocese of Rhode Island. Did you honestly think this would be the first time we'd be meeting?

Oh.

What?

I just…when we were talking earlier, you didn't mention you already knew him. I kind of wanted this to be

special.

It will be. Trust me.

"You don't have to get upset about this one," Satan said. "She volunteered."

"What are you talking about?"

"Check the trash."

Father Peña crossed the bedroom and glanced into the plastic bin. "What the…"

"Meet Mr Neepers. She made a blood sacrifice to summon me."

"I asked around about this girl; she's one of our youth ministry leaders. Why would she do something like that?"

"Because she wants to fuck the archdiocese's chief exorcist."

What are you doing?! I brought you here to help me seduce the cute priest, not embarrass me in front of him.

You wanted him to pay attention to you, right?

…

He's definitely paying attention now.

"See?" Satan said. "No need to feel guilty. Now why don't you come over here, and we can pick up where we left off last time?"

Father Peña looked at the door, like he was worried Becca's parents might come charging in at any moment. Finally, he took his glasses off and laid them on the dresser. "Last time was different. You were possessing me—"

"Yeah. To give you the best five-knuckle shuffle of your life."

Wait. What?

"We can't keep doing this," Father Peña sighed, sitting down on the edge of the mattress.

"Why not?"

"Because it's *wrong*. Because I'm violating my vow of celibacy with—" His voice dropped so low, Becca almost couldn't make out the words. "The Great Antichrist."

"No one needs to know."

"*He'll* know."

Father Peña pointed towards the ceiling.

"Trust me, he has more important things to worry about. Like people who fly Confederate flags off the backs of their trucks. And order eight baskets of breadsticks at the Olive Garden. Come on, how about a quickie for the road?"

"I don't know—"

This is bullshit.

Why? You're getting exactly what you wanted.

No, I'm not! This was supposed to be about my lustful desires, not yours. I never wanted to be the awkward third wheel. I can't believe I murdered Mr Neepers for this...

Fine.

"—And I think the Bishop's starting to get suspicious about how many demonic possessions have been popping up in Rhode Island—"

"Actually," Satan said, effortlessly dislocating a thumb to slip a wrist out of the restraints. "I think we've changed our mind."

"What?"

"You can walk out that door, and I'll let Becca here go. See you around—"

Wait!

Oh? Is there something you wanted, Becca?

Well, I mean . . . We can't let Mr Neepers' death be for nothing, right?

Of course not.

"Unless," Satan said, stretching out on the mattress like a *Hustler* centrefold. "You really wanted to. Who knows the next time I'll have such an *accommodating* host. But none of this 'we need to stop fucking around behind the Bishop's back' or 'the Catholic church would disapprove of my relationship with the Devil' nonsense. Either you're in or you're out."

Father Peña pushed them back against the pillows, his Dove Chocolate-brown eyes looking even sweeter than they had in the first row of the congregation. "Are you sure?"

Even with the ability to use her own voice, Becca just nodded.

"You know, if you'd just change your wicked ways," Father Peña said, brushing his nose against theirs. "We could probably see each other more often."

Satan reached up to run their fingers through Father Peña's messy shag of curls.

"You know, if you'd just punch a baby or two, we could probably see each other forever."

If I Only Had His Face

by Stephen Herczeg

I still can't believe we were such good friends for so many years.

Michael sat in a secluded spot at the far end of the high school grounds. He had made this his spot over many weeks. On discovering an old bench that had been discarded, he'd righted and cleaned it off so he could use it during lunch times. It sat in a remote shady spot, well away from the rest of the students. Well away from David and his newfound gang of friends.

Michael bit into his sandwich.

Ham and cheese. Again.

He munched mournfully as he watched David laughing and high-fiving his friends after he'd just made what seemed to be a hilarious joke. Even amongst his new coterie, Michael noticed that David stuck out. Taller, broader across the shoulders, and much better looking than any of the other boys he hung around with.

Those facts depressed Michael even more. His

shoulders slumped as he remembered.

Only a few years ago, he and David were the best of friends. Davey, Michael had always called him Davey, but even that had changed now. He and David had grown up together, went through the same elementary school, and then the same junior high together. Inseparable. On the weekends and after school, they were rarely apart. They liked the same toys, the same video games, the same TV shows. From the crack of dawn until dinner time, they could be found together. Even during school hours, they managed to gravitate towards each other and sit together. There was nothing weird about it—they were friends, pure and simple. The best of friends.

Then they started at Sanford High School. An overwhelming place filled with new faces and new experiences. Michael hated every minute. In the beginning, he would drag Davey away from this hellish place, so that at least he could be amongst one friend.

Then it started. For a while into that first year, they remained good friends. They hung out together during every spare moment they could find. But then slowly came the excuses. At first, Davey said he couldn't come around on weekends. Then he needed to stay back at school a little longer. Then came the sports, cutting into his spare time. Pretty soon, the amount they hung out together became less than their time apart.

The moment his friend said to call him David, Michael knew in his heart that their friendship had finished. It didn't take long after that for David to stop returning phone calls. They no longer sat near each other in class. They certainly didn't sit together at lunch anymore. After a year or so, they drifted towards different subjects, so they weren't even in the same classes anymore. On those rare occasions that Michael crossed David's path in the hallways, he'd look up into the taller boy's eyes, but David would turn away, refusing to lock eyes or even acknowledge his former friend's existence.

Michael wasn't cool.

David was cool.

David had his new friends. David had his sports. David had grown. Over the next couple of years, he shot up, filled out, and became gorgeous. Now, David had become the most popular guy in school. Every girl wanted to be with him. Every boy wanted to be like him.

Except Michael. Michael just wanted his friend back.

As he stared at the group, he began to realise more and more that the only way he could drag his friend away was to become more like David. That was never going to happen. David was tall. Michael was short. David was incredibly well built. Michael was still skinny, he'd never filled out, even though he'd tried. And David was handsome. Michael knew that even his mother would be hard pressed to describe him as handsome.

If only I had his face.

Michael turned his head away from his old friend and looked around the grounds. The cheerleaders were practising on the football oval. He peered around to make sure he wasn't being observed, then focused on their antics. The whole squad looked like the female equivalent of David and his crew. Each had athletic bodies with long shining hair framing pretty faces. They went through their more complex routines and ended up with a human pyramid—the climax of their performance at the Saturday night games.

At the apex of the pyramid, stood Carol. Blonde, beautiful Carol. Michael's heart had leapt when he'd first set eyes on her in his junior year. His heart melted again as he spied her. She had been cute, now she was downright stunning. He sighed. Like David's friendship, Carol's love was something that would never be his.

The girls' pyramid broke apart. Lunch time neared the end, and the cheerleaders responded with air kisses before going their separate ways. Michael watched Carol as she strolled towards the main school building.

Suddenly, she stopped and threw herself into David's

arms, mashing his face with a deep, passionate kiss. Michael's mouth dropped open.

That's new.

Deep inside, he felt a touch of rage, illuminated with an aura of jealousy. David's status had just simply peaked. He already had everything. Now he even had Carol.

Michael's shoulders slumped, and he looked down at his feet. He had nothing. No friends. No hope. Nothing.

His head turned towards the main school building as the siren sounded the end of the lunch period. His shoulders slumped further at the thought of another three hours of school. Gaining his feet, he slouched off towards the main doors.

Inside, Michael found the post-lunch hustle and bustle in full swing. He managed to reach his locker and swapped his lunch box for the stack of books he'd need for the afternoon's lessons. Realising he had to navigate the journey to the furthest classroom, he hurriedly turned and set off. He stopped short as he crashed into a mountain of hard muscle encased in a football jersey. His books toppled from his hands and sprayed out across the corridor floor.

Michael looked up into the eyes of his former friend. A smile spread across his face. "Davey?"

David's expression turned from stern to icy as he

stared back at Michael. A giggle floated in from Michael's left. He peered in that direction and found the blonde, slim cheerleader hanging off David's arm.

"Davey?" she said. "Who the hell's Davey?" She looked up at her boyfriend and asked, "Who is this guy? You gonna let him talk to you that way?"

David glanced at her for a moment, before turning back to Michael. His mouth curled up into a sneer as he said, "Why don't you watch where I'm walking?" Rather than wait for a reply, he simply pushed past Michael, dragging Carol with him, and headed off down the hallway.

Michael watched them walk away. He couldn't help it, but a small tear formed at the corner of his eye. He longed for his friend's companionship again, but at that moment, he realised nothing remained of his friendship with David.

The siren blew, signalling the start of the afternoon period.

"Shit," he said out loud before dropping to the floor and gathering his books.

***

Carol peered into the gloom and shivered. She pulled

David's letterman jacket tighter around her slight frame.

Where the hell is he?

She moved her wrist, trying to catch some light from the streetlight across the road to check the time. Her watch said six o'clock. The game starts at seven. She'd be late for cheerleader warmup. David would be late for his own warmup. He was never late, especially on game days. Carol sometimes thought he preferred it to her, but then they'd only been going together for a couple of months. Pretty soon, she'd allow his hands to wander a bit more freely on their off nights with no training or games. She hoped that would take his mind away from his sports.

A pair of headlights flashed in the dark as a car turned into her street. She saw a bleed of red paint as it approached and shivered again.

Thank God. I'm freezing.

The familiar red Mustang pulled up beside her. The interior was so dark, she could barely make out the driver, but it was David's car, so who else could it be? She popped the door open, but the interior light stayed off.

"Your light's broken, hon," she said. In the gloom she saw David nod, but he remained silent. "Well come on, we need to get moving." David simply sat still and stared towards her. Starting to feel frustrated, she raised her volume and said, "Come on. Move. We're late."

David reached towards her. "We don't have time for that now, we are really late. Get moving."

A sudden flash of lightning coupled with searing pain in her stomach and Carol's world went black.

***

As Carol's eyes blinked open, they slowly focused on her dimly lit surroundings. She tried to rub at her eyes, but her hands wouldn't move. She quickly looked down.

Carol found she sat on an old straight-backed wooden chair. Her hands were tied to the armrests with duct tape. She frantically pulled at the tape, but her arms wouldn't budge. She kicked out and found her ankles taped to the legs of the chair.

"Fuck," Carol said out loud. She thrashed at the bonds, throwing her body around as much as she could. The chair rocked and teetered, finally falling backwards. She hoped her weight would break the back of the chair. She only succeeded in driving the breath from her lungs and cracking her head on the backrest. Carol lay stunned for a moment, dragging breath back into her lungs and regretting her decision.

A chuckle emanated from the gloom at the far end of the room.

Carol looked around for the source. Then she saw the car. A red Mustang. David's car.

"David? David, this is not funny. Let me go. I'm not that sort of girl," she cried.

The laughing came louder. She heard footsteps crunch through grime on the concrete floor. Suddenly, someone dragged her into a sitting position, so that she stared back into the darkness at the far end of the room.

Her kidnapper stood behind her and spoke.

"That was a dumb thing to do. You won't be able to break your bonds, and you're not going anywhere, at least not yet," he said.

"Who? Who are you?"

"I'm you. I'm all those other people that hang around David."

"What?"

"Only a few years ago. I was all of you. I was David's whole world. But I called him Davey."

"I don't understand."

"I was Davey's best friend. We grew up together. Did everything together."

"I didn't know David had any other friends."

"Well, it seems he doesn't now. Thanks to you and your group. Since he started hanging around with all those other jocks, and you cheerleaders, he hasn't even thought of me."

Carol pulled at the bonds and turned her head around to see her assailant. His voice became louder. She realised he stood just behind her head. His face inches from her own. She could smell his breath and cringed at the foul odour.

"I know he's popular. I know he's the one to be around. I still want to be the one he hangs around, but I'm not cool enough. You people have poisoned his mind so much that he can't even stand to be near me anymore."

A picture flashed across Carol's mind. Walking down the corridor arm in arm with David. The short, skinny guy slamming into David. The guy that called him *Davey*. When she'd asked David about it, he became furious and told her to forget about it.

"It's you? The skinny kid with the books?"

"I'm touched. You remember me." The voice withdrew a little away from her. Carol breathed a sigh of relief. She'd been creeped out having him so close.

"You were friends with David? Sorry, Davey?"

"Yes. Lifelong buddies, or so I thought."

"You're new to the school? I don't think I've seen you around."

The voice amplified, almost shouting as he leaned close again. "Well, that's the problem, isn't it? I've been at that school for as long as Davey has, but no one knows who I am. No one notices me. I'm not athletic. I'm not popular. You and I have probably crossed paths dozens of times, but you couldn't even remember my face if you tried. Let's try, shall we? What colour is my hair?"

"Um, brown?" Carol said, desperately trying to remember more details.

"Wrong," Michael almost screamed. "It's black. The same colour as your boyfriend's." He stomped away from her. Carol heard a wooden crate, or something, go skittering across the room and crash into a wall as Michael kicked it. "I'm so sick of being insignificant. Sick to death of being ignored by you and all your group, but most of all I'm sick of having lost my best friend, just because he grew taller, stronger, and better looking."

The room went silent for a moment. Carol could hear heavy breathing. A chill ran up her spine. She tried to look around. She could see her tormentor's form behind her but couldn't make out any details. Suddenly, she felt his breath on her cheek again. She froze. Stared straight ahead. Pure terror swept across her.

"I worked it out, though. David doesn't like me the way I am. None of you do. So, I need to fit in. To do that, I need to be just like David. I need to have his car. I need to wear his clothes. I need to have his girlfriend. I need to have his face." The figure stepped away, grabbed Carol's face with his rough hands, and turned her head towards the red mustang. "So, I stole his car." Michael let go of her face; she grimaced at the pain as it dissipated. "Then I stole you." Fear bristled up Carol's spine.

He's gonna kill me?

A tear formed at the corner of her eye as the terror built up inside.

The boy stepped out from behind her and walked a few steps away. She saw he now wore a letterman jacket, like David's. She looked down at herself. He wore the jacket David gave her. It swam on his skinny body.

"I stole his clothes."

Fury started to overcome the fear within her. "That doesn't make you him. It's far too big for you. It makes you look foolish."

Michael laughed again. A strange staccato cackle. "But you haven't seen the best thing yet. The thing that makes me most like David. The thing that will make me popular enough to be accepted into your group. The thing that will make you mine. Will make me David."

Michael turned around, stepped forward, and dropped his head down to Carol's eye level. Now she recognised his features. They were more familiar than she imagined. They were the features she had grown to love over the last few months and had finally made them her own. She gagged back a throatfull of bile. A scream caught in her throat.

David's face stared back at her. David's face, but not on David's body. The eyes that stared out of David's face were not his. The mouth that spoke had a different voice.

"I knew the only way to become popular was if I had David's face."

Carol's scream burst forth.

"So, I stole that too."

We'll Always Have the Moon

by J.W. Garrett

Jeri left the meeting, a forced smile plastered on her lips. If she had to hold this expression much longer, her cheekbones might break. During a lull in the festivities, she escaped, heading straight to her inner sanctuary. "Nancy, absolutely no interruptions. Clear my schedule for the rest of the afternoon."

"As you wish, ma'am."

Pressing the button to shut the door firmly behind her, Jeri let out a low growl, then paced the length of her office and back again, not giving the expansive view of Earth from her desk a second glance. *I'll fix this. And soon. It's mine. He practically promised me.*

A soft tapping yanked her attention towards the door. *Nancy, damn her.*

"Jeri, it's me. Could we talk?"

Ugh…Darlene. "Sure. Just a sec." Letting an empty smile slide to her lips, she released a steadying breath. "Come on in."

Jeri lifted her eyes to Darlene's. Her energy and passion were so…genuine, matching the exuberant tilt of her lips. Hopefully, the gooey sweetness oozing from the woman wouldn't rub off on Jeri. "What can I do for you?"

"Look. This is hard…I get it. We're both well qualified for the CEO spot. I mean, second in command of the premiere company on the moon? We deserve it. But the boss chose me. Honestly, I'd probably be pissed too." She cocked her head. "Still, I don't want to lose your expertise. Can we get past it?"

Jeri held her breath, hoping she wouldn't bark out the laughter she was losing the battle to hide. *Get past it? Never. This woman…what an amateur.* This was only the beginning… "You got the position fair and square," Jeri lied. "Nothing to get past. Was there anything else?"

Darlene's brows knit in confusion, like she was disappointed no heart-to-heart would follow. "Well, all right. Let's bounce around some ideas tomorrow morning about where you'll plug in. You're *my* number one after all," she said, her face lighting with a flash of sparkly teeth.

Did the perfection of this woman never end? "I'll be there. Just see Nancy and add it to my calendar."

"Great. I've got so much to do. Not sure where to start just yet." Giddy, Darlene unleashed a nervous little laugh. "I'll leave you to your work."

Finally...

Jeri followed Darlene to the door, pushed the button, then watched it slide closed, as her mind raced, forming a plan.

Years had gone by since Jeri had touched the book inherited from her great-grandmother. Before she'd died, they had pored over the pages together, spending one indoctrinating summer deep in the practise of voodoo. But it had been so long ago, and Great Grannie was long dead. The book, however, was right where it belonged, with Jeri—one of only a few physical books she had brought with her when relocating to the moon, fulfilling a lifelong dream.

She hadn't used these spells in ages… In fact, she'd sworn off the practice. Once she'd secured the spot on the transport—when her company, Generations, had transferred to the moon—almost all her dreams had become reality. In comparison to that undertaking, this would be a breeze.

Her calendar cleared, Jeri had nothing preventing her from getting down to business now. With a wave and tight nod to Nancy—silently letting her know to keep her mouth shut—Jeri added, "Buzz me at home if anything urgent arises. Otherwise, I'll be in tomorrow morning."

A groove formed in her forehead as she recalled the steps from memory, while boarding the shuttle to the first residential settlement on the moon—her home. Already buried in the voodoo lore before she stepped inside her residence, Jeri shrugged out of her restrictive clothing and, in its place, donned a flowy top and skirt, freeing her arms and legs for movement.

At her bookcase, she let her finger glide along the small collection, creating a dusty trail in the wake of her search.

Her heart skipped a beat as she recognised the spine of the ancient book, steeped in knowledge of the craft. After yanking it free, Jeri plopped on her couch and crossed her legs. From the depths of her skirt pocket, she pulled out a voodoo doll, stickpins, and an amulet.

When she lifted the talisman and settled it in place around her neck, the powerful presence of her great-grandmother filled Jeri in waves. The dusty charm contained herbs and flowers last touched by her ancestor, its heavy aroma transporting her back to their last meeting, as her thoughts roamed.

I'll inflict her with something…an illness, nothing too horrible, just enough to incapacitate the woman. Then I'll have the chance to show my stuff—show the boss the error of his ways. By the time Darlene recovers, she'll

have lost out.

The spirit infused her, as if in a dream. She mumbled the incantation printed on the musty yellowed pages, and the song created by her words carried her away. The chant spilled from her lips, her body swaying to the rhythm only Jeri could hear. Her fingers trembled, holding the first stickpin, choosing the spot, then digging ever so slowly, twisting a path as she seated it deeply into the doll. But no more trembling came with the three other pins that followed, their placement effortless and certain.

Dragging the back of her hand across her forehead, she wiped away the sweat and curled into a ball and slept.

***

The atmosphere in the office had shifted overnight, a possible sign that Jeri's activities had paid off. A masked facade of serenity adorned her face, her gait confident as she blew by her assistant.

"Ma'am…Ma'am!"

"Yes, Nancy. What is it?"

"I thought it best you should know this right away." Nancy leaned in to whisper, as if the whole office didn't already know, judging from the dumbfounded looks around the place. "It's Darlene. She's been stricken with something. They're still testing, but it looks like she'll need to travel back to Earth soon, or she could…die." After spitting out the last word, Nancy shivered.

"How awful. What can we do?" Jeri remained fixed in place, hoping her shocked expression hit the mark. But death? That hadn't been Jeri's goal. Surely the hospital staff was mistaken. Jeri just needed Darlene out of the way for a while.

"I'm not sure there is anything." Nancy cleared her throat. "The boss wanted to see you upon your arrival."

"Sure. Whatever I can do. Let him know I'm on the way, after I drop my things in my office."

Minutes later the door to the president's office clicked shut, and as he rounded in his chair to face her, Jeri was almost too wired to stand still.

He lifted his chin. "Sit, Jeri, please."

"I heard about poor Darlene. What can I do to help?"

"I'm afraid there's nothing," he said, rubbing the back of his neck. "I take this as a sign. I should have given the position to you." He let out a deep sigh. "Such a difficult decision, but it's yours now, if you want it. This afternoon Darlene will take a medical shuttle back to Earth for treatment. They still don't know what's wrong with her, but she's quarantined, for everyone's safety, until they have more information."

"Dreadful circumstances. Of course. Anything I can do. I'm at your disposal."

"Good to hear 'cause I do need something right away."

"Name it."

"Darlene has documents, actual paper ones, that I need back before she leaves today. They're originals. I spoke with her early this morning before her condition worsened. Can you believe she was actually reading them, working from her hospital bed?"

"Wow! What a trooper. I'll head out now to get them."

Jeri watched while her new boss strode to the front of his desk and extended a hand. "Thank you, Jeri, and congratulations on your new position."

Rising, she clasped his palm, shaking it firmly. "Thank you. I'll get up to speed quickly," she said, already heading for the door, a smug smile playing around the corners of her mouth.

***

Jeri begrudgingly pulled a mask over her face. Wasn't she immune to her own spell? The medical staff had insisted though.

Pausing at the glass window in the door to the hospital

room, she drew in a breath. Darlene truly appeared as if she were at death's door. Jeri pushed through the door and dropped into the seat next to Darlene. "Hi, Darlene. I've come by for the paperwork and to wish you safe travels."

"Of course. Hand me my bag, will you?"

"No need. Aren't these the papers here? On top?"

"That's it."

Jeri folded the documents, then slid them into her purse.

Darlene grabbed her middle, moaning in pain.

"So sorry for all this, Darlene. Good luck to you. I'll be on my way so you can rest now."

Darlene nodded, her eyes filling with tears at her next gasp of pain.

Jeri strode for the door, yanking off her mask.

"Miss? Wait, Miss."

Two mask-clad nurses took Jeri aside before she'd cleared the door. "I'm sorry. You can't leave."

"Of course I can, you imbeciles."

"You just exposed yourself. Tests results have confirmed the virus the patient contracted is airborne. You're now infected. You need immediate treatment."

"What? No…"

"I'm sorry," one nurse said. "You'll need to travel to Earth as soon as possible. You'll be treated for pneumonic plague, along with Darlene."

The second nurse nodded and continued. "We're still trying to isolate how Darlene contracted the virus. Quite a few unknowns remain. I'm sorry. You'll need to prepare yourself in case the worst comes to pass."

"No, no, no. There's been a mistake." Pneumonic plague? She didn't even know how to do that with a spell. Did she? She'd just repeated the words from the book her great-grandmother had given her. What had she done wrong? Whatever it was, she needed her spell book to figure it out and reverse this mess so both of them would recover.

"Have a seat. We'll begin meds immediately. Darlene isn't responding to the drugs we've given her so far. We may be dealing with some mutated strain, more aggressive bacteria than what is found in pneumonic plague. Symptoms typically don't manifest this quickly."

"I can't. It's not possible. I have a new job. A job I've work so hard for. I need to go."

A sting pinched her arm.

Within seconds, her eyelids drooped. "No...You don't understand. I'm the best for the..."

***

Jeri woke, a dark chill invading the space around her. Her head buzzed; her stomach hurt. Even her hair ached. A soft hand found hers, the weak squeeze sending her into another bout of agony.

Great-grandmother? Help…

"Don't worry, Jeri," Darlene said, one hand over her heart, while the other gestured at the massive window, the majestic view of their temporary home winking at the pair as the shuttle soared closer towards Earth. "We'll always have the moon."

Oh, God…Shut her up. Can't someone please shut her up? No more dream job she had worked her whole life to obtain, no more strolls under the moon's first domed city, no more crater explorations, no more weightless playrooms, no more moon maid bots—all because of this woman beside her… *Idiot.*

"Jeri," the nurse called. "Jeri…Jeri."

Her words echoed, as if from far away.

"Deep breaths. We need to slow your heart rate. Jeri? Jer—"

Foreigner

by James Lipson

After three years of high school Spanish, Jake could barely manage *Where's the bathroom?* or *How are you doing?* These two phrases were far from enough to navigate a foreign city where everyone wants to kill you. It never crossed Jake's mind that his inability to speak another language would lead to his rebirth.

Jake hated his job, hadn't been in a real relationship in three years, and still lived with his parents. This would have been fine for a guy in his late teens, but on the south side of thirty, it was embarrassing and, more often than not, depressing.

A tropical holiday, filled with cheap booze, epic surf, and women in small bikinis was how his buddy Chris had proposed the trip to Playa Tamarindo, Costa Rica. Without hesitation, Jake agreed to the trip to the Nicoya Peninsula.

The holiday was originally planned for five guys, but, as usual, Chris dropped out—blaming *marital complications*—and Colin, once again, backed out due to lack of funds. In truth, Chris' wife was wildly insecure when it came to her husband, and Colin was still making payments on his third DUI. The remaining guys—Brian, TJ, and Jake—were forced to cancel the beachside hotel and downgrade to a motel several miles inland, away from the tourists and English-speaking residents. That necessitated a rental car, an unplanned expense.

They settled on Cartagena, which is in no way similar to its namesake in Columbia. This small town sits in the centre of a forgotten impact crater, a place where there is no reason to rush or traffic jams to avoid. Penniless surfers had obviously stayed in the town before, as no one paid particular attention to the three light-haired foreigners. For anyone on a wafer-thin budget who cared more about beer than beds, this town fit the cheaper bill.

Brian, TJ, and Jake surfed the glassy break for five near-perfect mornings of dawn patrol. The water was warm enough that wetsuits weren't required, even before sunrise. By 10 a.m., they grabbed lunch at a food stand (the cleanest of the four available each day), went back in the water for a few hours, then drove for an hour back to their motel room for an under-pressured, unsatisfying shower. Nights were spent in Cartagena, where they had their choice of two bars, although there were three. The third was in the garage of a local who thought he and his friends should have a place to drink on Sundays; the foreigners sensed it would be unwise to venture inside this one.

Opting to take the sixth day off from the morning surf, Jake, Brian, and TJ slept in past their regular dawn patrol time of 5 a.m. It was only a five-minute walk from the hotel to what could be considered the hub of Cartagena. The downtown district encompassed four retail shops, two restaurants, two bars, a closed barbershop, and a thrift store that never seemed to be open.

Lola's was the go-to choice for breakfast because the only other restaurant in town didn't open until 2 p.m. Six perfectly adorned tables that belied the exterior's dilapidated facade and a handcrafted coffee stand composed the sum total of Lola's. What it lacked in amenities, it more than made up for with the amazing food and baked goods that the current owner, Lucia, prepared fresh daily.

By 8:30, the pre-dawn work crowd had dispersed, and there was no waiting for a table. Instead of settling on a pastry and coffee for breakfast, Jake, Brian, and TJ spent the next hour and a half enjoying a large meal while waiting for the bar to open. The discussion, as usual, turned to favourite surf spots and slightly, if not greatly, exaggerated tales of conquered waves.

Never one to choose proximity over comfort or privacy, Jake took the opportunity to walk back to the hotel for his post-breakfast bathroom visit. Brian and TJ, now familiar with Jake's peculiar bathroom routine, wisely chose to meet him at the first bar which, shockingly, opened on time.

Jake considered ten in the morning far too early to start drinking, and in need of more alone time, he opted to wander around town before beginning to defile his slowly recovering body again. Most towns take on a different cadence just blocks away from Main Street, and Cartagena was no different.

Small, well-kept homes gave way to cramped quarters with owners who didn't prioritise cleanliness. By keeping the sun on his left, Jake ensured that he wandered in the same basic direction, though the winding streets and tangent alleys did their best to confuse him.

His last turn took him into an alley that somehow dimmed the sun more than he thought possible for this time of day. As his eyes struggled to adjust in the flat dusk, Jake thought he heard whispering, followed by footsteps that sounded as if they were breaking through iced-over snow.

He realised this was the first time he had been separated from TJ, the de facto translator for him and

Brian. It had never dawned on him, but without TJ, he had no effective way of communicating with anyone in town. Most people in Playa Tamarindo spoke English, but that was not the case in Cartagena. Absent tourists, there was no need for the locals to learn English.

Jake picked up his pace while checking his pockets for anything he could use as a weapon. The loose change and an old guitar pick would not do. Defenceless and feeling utterly exposed in the grey, he pleaded with his eyes to adjust to the low light. They were not in the mood to oblige as quickly as he would have liked.

Pride suddenly became far less important to him than his life. As fear overtook all rational thought, Jake bolted the remaining twenty murky yards to the end of the alley. The edge of the brick building clearly delineated light from dark as he approached the shadow-line like a hundred-metre sprinter. Jake exploded from the darkness and continued for a few yards before realising he was free from the alley.

Flush with cold sweat in the midday heat, Jake turned back to the darkness, hunched over with his hands on his knees, trying to fill his lungs, his gaze firmly affixed to the alley in anticipation of the challenge he knew was coming. Nothing nefarious or criminal emerged from the shadow. He was starting to feel more than a bit embarrassed, realising he had created the scenario in his head like he had as a child, afraid of the dark.

There was nothing special about this alley. The shadows were no different than those anywhere else; there was nothing malevolent about the area at all. He couldn't figure out why the back street had felt devoid of light only moments ago. Now he could clearly see through to the other side.

Recovered from what he assumed was a panic attack, Jake started in what he hoped was the direction of the bar. A peripheral movement caught his eye. He turned in time to witness the explosion—a momentary flash so intense it muted the sun. It made no noise, nor heat, nor shockwave. It was a colossal blast that made no apparent impact whatsoever.

***

Jake stared at the stars, wondering where he was, why it was nighttime, and why on earth he was lying on the street. Blinking his eyes to focus, he found himself on the same street off the alley. People were scattered about, obviously lying where they had been walking. Jake appeared to be the first to awaken.

The sparse streetlights feebly attempted to pierce the

night with tired bulbs that barely whispered. From the dark, he heard muttering, conspiratorial voices, prompting him to move away from the area. The lightly pulsating glow of what he hoped was downtown Cartagena became his beacon in the night.

For a few blocks, on both sides of the street, he witnessed people languidly awaking, equally confused as he had been moments earlier. They, too, looked lost and abandoned, unsure what had happened or exactly where they were. The now completely dark alley was also waking up; loud murmurs that seemed to grow exponentially in anger also grew in volume.

Jake broke into a full sprint without looking back. The voices had escaped the alley, and they remembered him. His pursuers were narrowing the gap as the end of the next street approached. Adrenaline-powered terror surged in Jake's rapidly depleting fuel tank, but he dug as deep as he could; he had to get away.

Head down, legs churning, arms pumping, his body (shockingly) remembered its high school track training with crisp and precise movements, Jake managed to put enough distance between himself and his pursuers that he no longer heard their footsteps or felt their threat.

Able to slow down but unable to get his bearings, Jake scanned left and right. Nothing looked familiar in the same area where he passed out. Everything seemed lower and smaller; the buildings, the trees, the streets took on a strange perspective that Jake couldn't make sense of.

As he approached the end of the street, everything appeared a little smaller. Unable to decide which direction to go at the T-shaped intersection, Jake scanned left and right. A single yellow bulb cast a feeble light next to the only road sign still vertical.

***

Jake couldn't decide. What if he chose wrong? Daunted, he lowered his head and could see the empty space between his feet. He was five feet off the ground and rising... Jake was flying. His heart pounded in his constricting throat. Still rising as he stared at the road shrinking below him, he ascended another ten feet before collapsing mid-air in pure exhaustion. Momentum carried him into the canopy of a large tree.

Completely bereft of energy, Jake clung to a large branch. Gasping for breath, he collapsed against the tree, relying on gravity to keep him on the bough. Jake had no idea what to think. His stomach made that decision for him, emptying itself onto the branches and ground below.

He stayed in the tree for a solid half-hour, slowly

coming around to the incredible truth: This was not a dream, and he was not hallucinating. He did, in fact, *fly*. Hidden in the treetop, Jake came face to face with the irrefutable truth of his new reality.

Unnoticed in his perch, Jake observed the people close by awaken as he had. Once the glassy, faraway look in their eyes dissipated, nearly every one of them demonstrated a new capability like Jake's (still incomprehensible) ability to fly. As more and more people arose, Jake witnessed a divergency of inconceivable feats.

With only the distant light from the streetlamp to see by, Jake witnessed a narrow microcosm of skills ranging from the bewildering ability to change skin colour to a meek little girl who froze a man solid in his tracks. (If the guy were still alive inside his ice tomb, no one would ever know.)

Jake watched as a woman attempted to walk through a wall of rock. She made it three-quarters of the way through before rematerialising. Jake convinced himself that her muffled screams were something else. His sanity depended on it.

Some of those who woke up, couldn't understand the mechanics of their new gift, if they noticed anything at all. A growing number of people did understand they had a new ability, one that would forever change their lives. Some of them wandered off, but they did so with newfound direction.

These new extrasensory gifts did not come without a cost. One by one, people pushed the limits of their powers, with the same results as Jake. They discovered they needed the energy of a long-distance runner, as opposed to just seeing it on TV.

Like Jake, each one tested these new gifts repeatedly, inevitably depleted to the verge of collapse. At this point, Jake felt calm enough to work his way out of the tree.

From the lowest branch that supported his weight, Jake dropped to the ground as silently as possible. As he descended, a twig caught him under his right arm, tearing off a small piece of his vintage Ocean Pacific terrycloth shirt. A week ago, ripping his favourite shirt would have seemed cataclysmic; today he couldn't remember why he had ever cared.

***

Jake's left foot landed nine inches higher than his right. Though the ground was level and clear of exposed roots, his feet landed in nearly ankle-breaking fashion.

Jake had struck an invisible object and landed hard,

falling and rolling to his right. Simultaneously, he heard a loud, close-by grunt. Incredibly, a man materialised under the tree. He was obviously waking up like everyone else.

Jake tried speaking to the man, who was utterly confused and afraid, attempting to calm him. Unable to understand English, the prone man watched in terror as his body flashed between visibility and invisibility. Obviously, he had no control of his new gift; the surging adrenaline was causing different parts of his body to appear and disappear at random like a wonky neon sign.

Desperate to get away from Jake, the man crab-walked backwards while clumsily reaching for something in his waistband. Not waiting to find out what it was, Jake found a broken brick to use as a weapon.

Jake grabbed the brick with his right hand and turned on the scuttling man. In his haste, the man's weapon got caught in his waistband. His eyes grew wide as Jake kicked aside the man's legs and fell on top of him, hoping to pin his arm between their bodies. Jake could feel the struggling man's trapped hand start to wiggle free. Jake had no choice; he swung the brick against the left side of the man's skull.

Protecting his head, the man blocked the incoming brick with the hand he had managed to release. Jake heard the crunch as the man's hand shattered. Instinctively recoiling, the man left his head unprotected. Jake seized the opportunity and crushed it with one adrenaline-fuelled swing. The wet, crunching sound of skull invading grey matter was nothing like you hear in action hero movies, though it was eerily familiar. It reminded him of the sound when he pulled his buried foot from the swirling redound of his favourite surf break back home.

The brick fell from Jake's hand, as his entire body shook violently. It felt like every cell was going to explode. Jake passed out again, unprotected for four full minutes near the only working lightbulb in the vicinity. This time when he awoke, the stars were in the same position. The dead man lay where he was struck, and the tree above him still clung to a piece of his shirt.

Jake couldn't help but notice that his legs were gone below the hem of his shorts. No thighs, no knees, no ankles, and certainly no feet or shoes. Constricting hysteria spread from his chest to where his legs should have been. Lifting his hand to his face, Jake saw nothing—and felt his head spinning from the shock. He had to get out of there!

Jake bolted up and ran as fast and as hard as he could. Sixty metres in, he was forced to slow to a brisk walk to regain his wind. Unbeknownst to him, he was walking seven feet off the ground.

Catching his breath, he settled back to the ground, tired but not thoroughly exhausted. Thankfully, he could now see all of his body parts. The realisation that he possessed the dead man's ability to disappear was almost as revelatory as his discovery that he could fly.

Jake felt energised by these newfound gifts and hoped to fine-tune them as quickly as possible. They exploded forth when he was terrified, but that wasn't reliable enough to get him through the night.

He made his way along the dirty street, trying to figure out how to become invisible. He found that if he concentrated hard enough, his hand would start to fade, just slightly.

Jake could only make himself appear blurry, as if his resolution was not equal to the rest of the world. It took less metabolic output to disappear than it did to fly. The two new skills, when combined, drained him exponentially faster than one by itself. Too fast, in fact. He popped back to full saturation as six people came around the corner.

They were all staring at him. "What?!" he shouted in bewildered irritation. There was only distant whispering that dispersed into the expanse. After a few tense moments, Jake heard a voice calling out instructions as the group advanced. Five people, not including the leader, separated from each other with an eerie equidistance. Jake didn't wait to figure out their intentions; he turned around and ran.

Fright and anger propelled him, and he began to fade at the same time he gained elevation. Exerting this much energy on both flying and vanishing would deplete him within seconds. He knew he couldn't last in the air much longer.

Just high enough to land on the roof of one of the smaller buildings, he veered right and touched down on a flat two-storey structure. Landing hard, exhausted and sweaty, Jake crawled as quietly as possible to look over the edge. Four people ran past as a fifth glided silently behind them. None noticed that he had gone in the one direction they didn't think to look…up.

Jake fell back against the roof, drank in the night air, and stared at the moonless sky. He reflected on his favourite childhood superhero comics. He had come to realise that flying wasn't as glamorous as Superman made it out to be. Keeping his balance in 3D space was unimaginably difficult; the undue stamina it took to remain aloft was Herculean.

His breathing back to normal, Jake sat up and glanced over the edge. A young woman with eyes that glowed an unreal shade of amber was silently staring at him. How she found his hiding spot, Jake would never know.

They stared at each other for a few moments before a green bolt of energy exploded from her left, blasting her backwards fifteen feet. The force was so violent that it caused her to somersault twice before she landed on her side in silent repose. Her right arm was bent at a grotesque angle. Refocusing her gaze upon Jake, the amber light from her eyes faded to black as a fine mist rose from her body. The pulsating cloud migrated to the source of the blast, the rightful heir to the girl's powers.

The energy travelled to a solitary figure standing in the middle of the street. Jake saw him drop to the ground as the black cloud invaded his body. Jake was witnessing the transference of power. Energy can't simply dissipate; it lives on within a new host.

Jake did not want to be there when that individual awoke, so he quietly made his way to the front of the building. He peeked over the ledge onto Main Street. Only four of the nine lights functioned, and two of those were blinking sporadically. On the right wall, Jake saw a pipe running the length of the building, disappearing behind a truck on its way to the sidewalk and drainage parts unknown.

Hoping the pipe was anchored sufficiently to hold his

weight for the few seconds it would take to shimmy down, Jake swung his leg over the edge and started his descent. Halfway down, the telltale sounds of bolts pulling free from cheap concrete foretold his future.

Jake didn't wait to test the strength of the remaining bolts. He let go, expecting to land feet first on the hood of the truck. Momentarily forgetting he could fly, he was shocked to find himself smoothly floating, staring at the rusted pipe that was now two feet from the wall.

Jake gently lowered onto to the hood, touching down with a surfer's grace and balance. Immediately sliding off the driver's side fender, Jake was relieved to be back on the ground. Hidden twelve feet behind the old truck, someone yelled, "Oye!"

Jake shifted towards the passenger's side between the door and the wall, crouching to hide in the truck's shadow.

"*Que tal?*" another voice retorted.

Realising the disembodied voices weren't speaking to him, and more than likely had never seen him, Jake let himself relax slightly. From his position between the truck and the building, Jake witnessed a fight like none he had ever seen.

The man from the right moved so quickly, Jake wasn't sure anything had happened, until he saw him abruptly crumple before the second man. His severely broken hand was hanging uselessly from his wrist.

On his knees, writhing in pain, the first man never saw what stopped him. Jake did. The second man casually walked around a fading, shimmering plane that looked like floating glass. He took out a gun and shot the first man in the back of the head.

Standing over the dead man, the shooter collapsed onto the sidewalk. Jake made his decision in a microsecond. Springing out of the darkness, he wrestled the gun from the prone man's hand and with trembling fingers pulled the trigger.

Jake didn't pass out this time. He was acutely aware as both men's energies escaped their lifeless bodies and merged with his. He felt like he was holding a knife in an outlet, and he wanted to jam it in even deeper.

His capabilities were expanding, and he needed more. Turning towards the alley, Jake's eyes adjusted as he rose into the air, gazing down upon his own Serengeti and the prey that would soon be his.

Eternal Reflection

by Jessica Chanese

Death did little to temper Ephraim's hatred for Orin. His afterlife was consumed with ensuring his brother, and those he loved, suffered greatly. For Ephraim, a lifetime of coveting all Orin had and was had given way to an eternity of seeking retribution.

As Ephraim saw it, Orin had stolen everything from him—his fortune, his title, his betrothed. Anything the former Duke had ever valued was taken away by his younger brother. Ephraim had never fully comprehended why Orin was so favoured by the world at large, and he'd be damned if Orin's legacy would overshadow his own.

Many in their small town believed Ephraim had been cruel and calculating when he was alive. Where Orin was kind and noble, Ephraim was callous at best, sinister at worst. Some whispered that Ephraim's cruelty verged on sadism. Rumour had it that there were a number of prostitutes who could validate the speculation around Ephraim's violent proclivities, but who kept their stories close for fear of reprisal.

Ephraim paid well to indulge his darker urges. There

were few women who would willingly give themselves over to him, while Orin found himself with an endless supply of eager female companions.

Women who wouldn't waste breath on a passing hello to Ephraim would risk impropriety to stop Orin on the street, inviting him to join them for drinks or a walk in the park. Women from prominent families with wealth and good looks to spare would practically shed their gowns when Orin glanced their way across a ballroom.

Women like Calla.

Ephraim remembered how Calla's complexion flushed and her eyes brightened when Orin took her hand in introduction at a gala one evening. Her reaction was typical; it was Orin's demeanour upon meeting Calla that struck Ephraim as noteworthy.

His normally silver-tongued brother stumbled over his own name when his eyes found Calla's, and Ephraim knew no other woman would capture Orin's attention that night or any night which followed. It was this realisation that made Calla an invaluable prize for Ephraim.

It hadn't mattered that Orin was ready to put bachelorhood behind him for Calla or that Calla was hopelessly enamoured with Orin. Ephraim made sure she would be his, no matter how fiercely she recoiled at his touch or how sorrowful her cries on the night her father

signed the betrothal agreement.

The instant Ephraim understood Orin's interest in Calla was more than fleeting, he had tracked down Calla's father and offered him a sum of money greater than everything the old man had earned in his lifetime.

It didn't matter that Orin was more handsome or more courageous. It was irrelevant that even their mother didn't bother to hide her preference for Orin. As the eldest son, Ephraim controlled their family's fortune. It was Ephraim's name on the deed of their estate, Ephraim's signature on the pay cheques of half the townspeople, Ephraim's name amended by *Duke of Bellingham* after his father's passing.

But, it was Orin's name Calla screamed when Ephraim tired of waiting for her to succumb to him. It was Orin's arms she rushed into when he stormed into the room.

"What in the hell are you doing?" Orin demanded. He held Calla close and stared down at his brother with obvious disgust.

Indignant, Ephraim left his saviour brother and petulant betrothed in pursuit of an outlet for his frustrations.

What was he doing? What was he doing? Taking what's mine to take, dammit, Ephraim fumed.

Orin could never understand what it was like to have

women cringe when he stood too close. Orin never *had* to take because everything was given to him freely.

Ephraim didn't intend to snap the servant girl's neck. Years of having to take or pay for what was offered willingly to Orin, capped off by Calla's rejection, had worn down his patience.

His restraint slipped. When the servant girl fought and screamed, Ephraim squeezed her throat only to quiet her. It wasn't *his* fault she was so fragile that he severed her spinal cord instead.

For the second time that evening, Orin barged into a room his brother occupied after hearing a woman's screams. Calla followed close behind, shrieking when she took in the macabre tableau waiting for them.

Ephraim crouched on the kitchen floor, examining the dead girl's body without emotion. The girl, barely a teenager, stared at the ceiling with glassy eyes, the terror of her final moments plain on her pale face.

Orin had no words this time, just silent rage as his fist hammered into Ephraim's temple. Ephraim registered confusion—*why did Orin care about the life of a worthless serving girl anyway?*—just before he fell into unconsciousness.

***

Bystanders spat in Ephraim's face and called Orin honourable when he handed Ephraim over to Constable Cross. Calla stood hand in hand with Orin, her eyes cold as the constable bound his prisoner's hands and feet, then shoved him into his carriage.

Ephraim didn't survive long enough for a trial. The servant girl's brothers intercepted the constable's carriage on its way to the jailhouse. The constable gladly disappeared into the woods to take a piss—and to give the men time to take their vengeance.

Ephraim's remains were so disfigured when Constable Cross returned to the carriage that no one would question his claim of a rabid animal attack on the shackled prisoner while he answered nature's call.

Not that anyone cared to second-guess the lawman's story. Consensus amongst the townspeople was Ephraim got only a fraction of what he deserved, and no one cared if it was a wild dog, three distraught men avenging their dead sister, or a bevy of winged pigs with horns that gave it to him.

***

Ephraim's spirit lingered after the constable's men disposed of his battered body. While some detained spirits avenge their deaths by attacking their murderers, Ephraim wasted no time on the simple men who caused his physical demise. He knew it was Orin who caused his death, just as it had been Orin who ruined his life.

Only hours after his death, Ephraim's spirit began a relentless campaign to torture Orin's psyche to madness.

"You will never be rid of me, brother," Ephraim's voice whispered in Orin's mind as he lay down to sleep that night, and each night after.

When Orin stood in front of the bathroom mirror to shave the next morning, he swore he saw Ephraim's dark eyes and malevolent smile flash in the glass before him. He caught sight of him again later that day, when Ephraim's transparent form materialised behind Calla, leering as she kissed Orin with a passion she had never shown her deceased betrothed.

Ephraim haunted Orin with zealous determination, day in and day out, for months on end. Orin told his beloved Calla what was happening; how it felt as if his grip on reality was slipping further away each time he heard his dead brother's voice or saw flashes of his image.

"It's not real," Calla would reassure him. "He's gone, Orin."

Orin would nod, but he knew Calla was wrong. He knew it was Ephraim's taunting voice telling him the servant girl would be alive if he hadn't interfered with Ephraim taking what was rightfully his. It was Ephraim's menacing shadow lurking in the corners of the bedroom when Orin made love to his new wife, Ephraim's jeers searing into Orin's brain when he lay beside Calla afterwards.

It took him more than a year, but finally, Ephraim succeeded in crushing his brother's will to live. Orin could no longer withstand the unyielding assaults from Ephraim's ghost, and he believed his brother's spirit when it said the world would be better off without him in it. That Calla would have a chance at a better life if she wasn't weighed down by Orin's worthlessness.

Ephraim's spirit gloated as Orin huddled in the clawfoot tub and drew the razor along his wrists.

It was Ephraim's cackle bouncing through the house that brought Calla running into the upstairs bathroom. She rushed to Orin's side, checking for any sign Ephraim hadn't finally succeeded in destroying the only man she ever loved.

Ephraim watched as his brother's soul rose from his body, answering a call that hadn't beckoned Ephraim on the day of his death. It was just another injustice Ephraim had to endure on account of Orin.

Calla jumped to her feet, shouting at her unseen

enemy. "I know you're here, you evil bastard! I know you did this. And you will pay."

Ephraim chuckled darkly to himself, certain a creature as useless as Calla could do nothing to him.

***

Calla entered the small cottage behind the apothecary's shop. She found the apothecary's daughter, Denna, busy chopping herbs. The young woman had a reputation for dabbling in the darker arts on the fringes of her father's business.

"I need something to take care of an evil spirit," Calla said.

"Take care of?" Denna raised an eyebrow but kept her eyes on the knife she wielded as it bit through stems and stalks.

"Punish. Forever."

The young witch stopped her preparations. "It'll cost you."

"Whatever the expense, it's worth it," Calla said flatly, but Denna saw the fire flash in her eyes.

***

Calla left Denna's cottage with a small oval mirror with a black-lacquered frame wrapped carefully in brown paper. Tucked inside was a squat black candle, a packet of incense, and a notecard on which a binding hex was written in Denna's neat script.

Denna's instructions echoed in Calla's mind as the time to act drew near.

"On the night of the next new moon, place the mirror on the floor of the room where the spirit lingers. Light the candle on its surface and burn the incense in each of the room's four corners. Then say the words, and it will be done. Never to be undone."

And so, on the night of the next new moon, Calla did as Denna said. She read the hex's words aloud and watched as the black candle's flame flickered and grew, stretching into a column almost as high as the ceiling. The air grew heavy, the incense's fragrance near suffocating, and the room was black except for the blaze's glow. Calla gasped as Ephraim's image came into focus in the core of the flames.

The terror in Ephraim's expression as his spirit was pulled from the flames and into the mirror filled Calla with righteous satisfaction. When it was done, the candle flame withdrew and extinguished. Calla tentatively reached for the mirror. Finding it cool to the touch, she picked it up, examining its surface. Calla caught one more glimpse of Ephraim's horrified face before his image faded into the glass, which was now his spirit's permanent home.

***

Calla gave birth to a son six months after Orin's passing. She laboured in her bedroom, and when it was done, the doctor laid her newborn in her arms.

"What shall we call the boy?"

Calla looked over the doctor's shoulder at the small oval mirror hanging on the opposite wall.

"Orin, of course," she said. "After his father. He will carry on his family name and legacy."

When Calla was ready to take lovers again, she made sure the mirror was positioned so that Ephraim's ghost was forced to watch as she pleasured her bed mates. To watch as she moaned in answer to their touch. To watch as they lost themselves to waves of release Ephraim would never know again.

In time, Orin Jr grew old enough to ask about his father. Calla pulled him into her lap in a rocking chair in her bedchamber. She glanced frequently at the oval mirror as she regaled him with stories of his father's kindness, bravery, and strength.

"Did Papa have any brothers or sisters, Mama?" the boy asked.

"No, dear. Your father was an only child." Calla fixed her stare on the mirror. "You may hear tales about a man once believed to be his brother. They are wrong. That man was nothing but a shadow of your father, and he could never be any more."

When Orin Jr was a grown man with children of his own and Calla knew her days on Earth were drawing to a close, she asked her son to bring her to their family's mausoleum. Calla wanted to watch for herself as the mirror entrapping Ephraim's spirit was affixed on the inside wall just above the entrance.

Calla, who knew such sorrow in life, would know only peace in death. While her spirit would re-join her late husband's, Ephraim's ghost would spend eternity watching countless outpourings of love and admiration by mourners who visited Calla and Orin's graves.

Mourners who would never know the name of the spirit ensnared in the oval mirror.

 Til Death Don't Us Part

by Jodi Jensen

Owen buried her in the garden, next to the peas. They'd been her favourite, and he hoped she'd rest easy here.

"Sweetheart?"

The whispered word drifted into his ear. He speared the shovel deep into the ground and leaned on the handle, his heart heavy and his soul weary. "Yes, Lydia?" The words came out as broken and tattered as he felt.

"Come inside, before someone sees you."

He glanced around and saw nothing but field after field, dirt roads, and his two-storey farmhouse in the distance. "No one can see," he muttered. "No one will know."

"Someone can always see," she insisted. "Please, come inside."

Something inside of him snapped.

He snatched the shovel and spun around, brandishing it like a bat. "You need to stop!" he growled. Gripping the wooden handle with both hands, he took a swing, then crumpled to the ground in a defeated heap as the shovel passed right through the ghostly form of his late first wife. "You need to stop," he sobbed.

"No, *you stop*," she countered.

* * *

Eight months earlier...

"I think we should move in together."

"What?" Owen did a double take from the kitchen table, where he sat reading the morning newspaper. "Chloe, no—"

"Why not? Don't you want to do this every morning?" Chloe laid a manicured hand on his arm and squeezed. The sunlight streamed in through the window, lighting her face as she smiled hopefully at him.

He set his coffee cup down and put his hand on top of hers. "I have the farm to take care of." Even as he said it, he knew it sounded lame, but it was the only thing he could say under the circumstances. "I can't just leave my crops and animals. That's my livelihood."

"I know that." She giggled and pulled her hand away, giving him a playful slap on the shoulder. "I mean, I could move in with you at the farm. What do you think?"

Owen tore his gaze from hers and looked back at the paper. The words in front of him blurred into jumbled nonsense, much like the ones in his head. "That's…not possible."

"Oh…" Chloe got up from the table and leaned against the counter, her eyes narrowed at him. "And why is that?"

"I can't—there're things—" He searched for the right words to make her understand and came up woefully short. There was simply no way to explain Lydia. "Look, what we have here, right now, this is good. Can't we just keep it this way?"

Even as he said it though, he knew it wasn't going to work. Now that she'd asked, and he'd refused, there was no going back to the way it was a few minutes ago.

"You know, now that I think about it, I've never been to your place. Not even once. What aren't you telling me? Are you married or something?" When he didn't answer right away, Chloe exploded from where she stood and stormed across the room. "That's it, isn't it? You're married!" She yanked the door open and glared at him. "Get out!"

Rising from the table, Owen sighed. That wasn't it, not exactly anyway, but it was easier to let her think that.

He grabbed his jacket and walked out into the crisp morning air, resigned to never seeing her again.

It didn't last long.

A month later, she showed up at his door, suitcase in hand.

"What're you doing?" Owen looked over her shoulder and saw her car packed to overflowing. She even had boxes strapped to the roof. "Chloe?"

"You never answered me before." Her gaze locked on his. "Are you married?"

"Not exactly, I mean—"

"Cut the crap, Owen. Yes or no?" A muscle in her jaw twitched, and she spoke between clenched teeth. "Do you have a wife?"

"No," he sighed, praying Lydia was nowhere near. "Not anymore."

Chloe's eyes filled with tears. "Then you have to let me stay here." Her voice choked up. "I'm pregnant."

Owen stumbled backwards, his head reeling. *Pregnant?* Concerns about Lydia fled momentarily as he stared at Chloe's belly. "Are you sure?" He heard the tremor in his voice…and the hope. "I thought you said you couldn't—"

"I didn't think I could." She took a hesitant step towards him. "Are you—happy?"

"My God," he whispered. "A second chance."

Her brow crinkled at his words. "Owen?"

"Happy—yes, I'm happy," he assured her.

"That's good, because there's more." She held out a piece of paper. "I've been evicted."

Owen scrubbed his hand through his hair. "What? Why?"

"The landlord's daughter needed a place to stay." Chloe held out a piece of paper.

"Notice to vacate," he muttered as his eyes scanned the pink slip. "Three days—wait, this was over a week ago! Where've you been staying?"

"Can I come in or what?" She wiped a hand under her eyes to stem the flow of tears and sniffled. "Please."

Owen sighed and opened the door wide. As Chloe stepped over the threshold, he took a quick glance around the living room, but didn't see Lydia. He wasn't relieved at all though, in fact, he'd have felt better if he knew where she was.

Chloe set her bag by the fireplace and picked up a picture off the mantel. "Is this her? Your first wife?"

Hurrying across the room, Owen took the picture from her and put it back without looking at it. "Chloe—"

"Don't say it." She spun to face him. "Don't tell me I can't stay here. I'm carrying your child and I've got nowhere else to go."

"I'll pay to get you into a new place—"

"Don't be stupid, babe, it'll be fine. You'll see." She tucked a dark brown strand of hair behind her ear and stepped close, wrapping her arms around his waist. "Please, let's just try."

Against his better judgement, Owen pulled her closer and rested his chin atop her head. "Okay, hun, you can stay."

As Chloe squealed in delight and uttered muffled words of thanks into the front of his shirt, Owen caught sight of a movement in the corner.

Lydia.

Her lips tightened into a thin, angry line and she shook her head, her ghostly form vanishing in a swirl of smoky black wisps.

* * *

Later that night, Owen woke with a start. He cocked his head to the side and blinked into the darkness, trying to determine what had woken him. Beside him, a figure under the blankets stirred, and he had a moment of panic.

Ah, yes. Chloe.

He crept out of bed and went downstairs for a glass

of water.

"Get rid of her."

Owen issued a bone-weary sigh. "You woke me to tell me that?"

"I mean it. Get rid of her or I will."

"Maybe it's time for us both to move on. I mean, you died—"

"And whose fault was that?" she snapped.

He gripped the edge of the sink with both hands and stared at the chipped porcelain in the bottom. "I did eve—"

"Everything you could," she mimicked, her voice thick with disdain. "Save it. If I'm stuck with you, then you're stuck with me. Get. Rid. Of. Her."

He turned and faced his dead wife. "I can't."

Lydia crossed her arms over her chest. "And why not, pray tell?"

Owen looked at the floor. "She's pregnant," he whispered.

His statement was met with silence and he glanced up, only to find himself alone in the kitchen. His breath caught in his throat.

Chloe!

Taking the stairs two at a time, he raced to the bedroom.

Lydia stood by the edge of the bed, her lips twisted,

and eyes narrowed as she focused on Chloe's sleeping form. "She can stay…for now."

"What?" Owen did a double-take, studying Lydia's inscrutable expression.

She spared him a glance, her eyes nothing more than two inky black spots. "You heard me." Her gaze returned to the bed, and with a wave of her hand, the blankets folded over to Owen's side, leaving Chloe uncovered. Lydia crouched by the side of the bed, her face inches from Chloe's barely discernible baby bulge. "She can stay."

Before he had the chance to respond, Lydia disappeared, leaving behind black wisps that caressed Chloe's belly.

* * *

Owen had never juggled two women before, but as the days turned into weeks, and then, months, things fell into an uneasy routine.

Lydia stayed out of sight during the day, but invaded Chloe's dreams nightly. Chloe would wake, damp with sweat and trembling as she recounted the nightmare to Owen.

It was the same every time. A figure would step from

the shadows of their bedroom, dark gaze glued to Chloe's ever swelling stomach. As the apparition approached the bed, arms outstretched, its fingers twitched. The hands and arms turned into wispy tendrils that reached inside her belly.

Chloe lay frozen, afraid to cry out, unable to move as the creature's face morphed into that of a lovely young woman. With deliberate strokes, the woman caressed and cradled the baby in Chloe's womb while humming softly.

The closer they got to the due date, the more disturbed Chloe was, until late one night, as she lay sleeping, the situation shattered into chaos.

"Get away from me!"

Owen threw back the blankets and scrambled out of bed, unsure if it was Chloe's flailing limbs or her anguished screams that woke him this time. "Babe, you okay?"

She kicked at something he couldn't see, and her head thrashed side to side. "No, no, no—NO!"

Owen leaned over, grabbed her shoulder, and shook vigorously. "Chloe! Wake up!"

She shoved his arm away, and he stumbled back from the force of it. Her face contorted into a tortured expression with deep frown lines marking her forehead. Lips twisting into an ugly sneer, her hands punched wildly into the darkness, connecting with nothing. "Get the fuck away!"

Not knowing what else to do, he snatched the glass of water from her nightstand and splashed it on her face. "Chloe!"

She sputtered and coughed as her eyelids flew open. Her gaze darted around the room, then landed on Owen. She collapsed against him, her fingers clawing at his back. "My baby, my baby," she sobbed. "She stole my baby."

"Shhh…" He rocked her back and forth, one hand resting on her swollen baby bump. "It's okay, I'm here. No one stole him."

Chloe jerked away from him, her eyes wide and panicked. "She did! I saw her, *felt her* yank him right from my belly." Her hands curled protectively around her middle as tears streamed down her cheeks. "She took him."

"Who?" He attempted to gather her in his arms again.

Her jaw tightened, and she spat the word from between clenched teeth. "Lydia."

Owen's breath caught in his throat. "What? Why would you say—"

"She told me," Chloe yelled. "She told me everything! How she died, how your baby daughter died." She paused to glare at him. "How you did *nothing* to stop it.”

He scrubbed a hand through his hair and took several deep breaths to calm his anger. “You don’t know what you’re talking about.”

“Because *you* were too busy, working in your precious fields to take her to the hospital,” Chloe accused, her breaths coming in heavy pants.

“Enough!” he roared. He paced the room, trying to get himself under control before he spoke. Finally, he stopped in front of her. “I couldn’t have known she’d go into labour three months early. Nor that her water would break while I was out working. It had already happened by the time I got home. They were both gone and there wasn’t a fucking thing I could do.”

Chloe opened her mouth to speak again, but nothing came out. Instead, her lips formed a perfect “O,” and she glanced down.

Following her gaze, Owen saw wetness spreading from underneath her. His heart pounded as he took a step closer. “Is that—”

“My water—” she whispered.

He grabbed his cell and called an ambulance.

* * *

"Stop trying to replace me." Lydia vanished in a swirl of smoky black wisps.

Owen shuddered. He knew where she'd gone, back to the only place she *could* go. He sat alone in the dirt, staring at Chloe's grave until the sun sank low in the sky, then clambered to his feet and trudged towards the house. The wooden steps creaked as he trod heavily on each one, echoing the reluctance in every fibre of his being. He paused, one hand on the doorknob. Had it not been for his newborn son, he'd burn this place down and be done with it. Done with *her*.

He opened the door and his broken heart twinged at the sight that greeted him. In the fading light of day, with the curtains drawn, Lydia sat in the corner rocking chair, the baby cradled in her arms.

They almost looked real, almost looked alive.

With one flip of the living-room light switch, his heart plummeted.

He stared at his new reality, his infant son, forever in the care of the one who'd stolen him.

"I named him Oliver." Lydia stroked the tiny head, her lips curving into a smile. "He has your chin."

Owen bristled. "His name is Matthew, after Chloe's father. It's what she wanted. Or are you going to take that from her, too?"

Lydia shot him a dirty look. "Matthew Oliver then, and I told you to get rid of her. Chloe's death is on you, just like mine is."

"Don't you put this on me," he ground out. "Chloe died because of *you,* took that whole bottle of pills because of what *you* did."

She lowered her gaze to Matthew and smiled sweetly. "That's what daddy does, baby boy. He buries his wives and children."

Don't lose it, don't lose it, don't—

"Not going to argue that, are you?" Lydia smirked.

Owen turned away.

"Don't you want to see your son?"

Closing his eyes, Owen saw Matthew clearly. Ten fingers, ten toes, a head topped with soft brown fuzz. Cherub lips that would never utter a single cry, long-lashed eyelids that would never open. A tiny, perfect chest that would never rise and fall with a breath.

Born sleeping.

That's how the doctor had referred to the stillborn baby.

But Owen knew the truth. Knew what Lydia had done. And he hadn't been able to do a damn thing to stop it.

"I've seen enough," he said in a half-strangled

whisper. He dragged himself upstairs and sat on the edge of his bed.

The bed he'd shared with Chloe.

He'd already shed so many tears, he didn't think he had anymore, yet still they fell. But as they did, his anger grew, blooming, pressing him to do something, anything, to stop this madness once and for all.

An idea popped into his head, and before he changed his mind, he hurried to the closet for the lamp oil stored high on the shelf. Next to that lay his pistol.

Grabbing both, he returned to the bed, dousing it with the lamp oil. He set the empty bottle on his dresser, then took the plain gold band he'd worn while married to Lydia out of his pants pocket. Careful to keep the ring out of sight, he placed it behind the bottle and covered it with a worn handkerchief.

He turned back to the bed and sat on the edge of the mattress, pistol in hand. "Lydia!"

Her ghostly figure emerged from the darkest corner of the room. "You don't have to yell, I'm right here."

"Where's Matthew?"

"Sleeping, or he was, until you hollered loud enough to wake the dead." She laughed at her own joke.

"That's not funny," he snapped. "Why? Why'd you take him?"

"Don't play dumb, you know why." She tilted her head as she regarded him through narrowed eyes. "I wanted him, of course, and besides, you owed me a child."

"But why? Why didn't you keep our daughter?" He kept his gaze fixed on her, wishing he could burn her with the hatred he felt. "Why'd you have to take my son?"

Lydia laughed, a dark, ugly sound that made him shudder. "Our beautiful girl died *before* I did, she'd already gone into the light by the time I joined her in death."

Owen shook his head. "Damn you to hell, you evil, jealous bitch." He put the pistol to his temple. "You wanted something that wasn't yours and you just took him, and to hell with the consequences."

Lydia gave him a peculiar smile. "Go on then, do it. You'll be stuck with me forever."

"That's what you think." His lips twisted in a sly smirk, and he pulled the trigger.

The bed erupted in flames as Owen's spirit shot from his body. In a flash, he was downstairs, Matthew in his arms.

"Give him back!" Lydia screeched from the top of the stairs.

Ignoring her screams, he dashed outside with his son

and stood at the edge of the field as his house was consumed by the fire.

She followed him to the front door, then jerked forward, straining against a barrier she couldn't see, unable to leave the house. "What've you done? Owen!" She banged against the doorframe to no avail. She was well and truly anchored by the wedding ring, same as she'd been since her death, only she'd never realised it.

He'd figured it out though and had tested his theory by carrying the ring in his pocket when he buried poor Chloe in the garden.

Owen watched as the ghostly form of his late wife faded into black wisps that blended with the fire, and for the first time in years, was free.

Heart's Desire

by Stacey Jaine McIntosh

I had always wanted what I couldn't have. Being cursed made it that much worse. But as a child, it had been limited to toys and games. Tantrums and tears ensured I got my heart's desire.

Now that I was grown, it wasn't so simple.

When my sisters got jewels to adorn their necks and I got nothing, jealously reared its ugly head. Envy ruled my days and nights. I couldn't switch off. The feeling ate at me. Gnawing away until one day, I took a blade to the offending sister's neck and took those jewels for my very own.

Not Mine

by Jo Niederhoff

Michael Kelly was one lucky son of a bitch.

I say *was* because…well, you can probably guess why. Sometimes I feel a little bad I can't talk about it in the present tense, but never for very long. You see, I used to envy him. Hell, everyone did. Even people who didn't know much about him would wish they could be like him. He had this air of contentment, of having exactly what he wanted, and even if you didn't know about the money, the houses, the adoring boyfriend his conservative family just accepted, you'd feel that little ache inside you. *Look at that asshole,* it said. *What does he have that I don't?*

Well, he had money for one thing. He had a couple houses scattered around the country. He had that boyfriend, and even though I'm not into guys, I would have died happy if he'd just given me a smile half as stunning as the ones he gave Michael.

Dale. That was his name. It never really stuck in my head, for some reason.

To tell the truth, sometimes I still envy Michael. Not as he is, of course, but as he was. As he always will be to some people. They talk about him like his misfortune never hit, like he never had anything bad happen at all.

No one will ever talk about me that way.

But that's all right. I envy him, but only a little bit. Why would I need to feel that ache now? He's lost everything but his reputation, and I have everything he's ever had.

***

Back when Michael was still lucky, I'd ask him how he managed to get everything so easily.

"I didn't get it," he said, idly swirling his wine glass. "Not the way you think."

"But it's all yours," I said. "Things don't just fall out of the sky."

"The meteor did."

Right. The meteor that he managed to sell to a science museum. According to him, they just wouldn't take it as a donation and insisted he accept some form of payment. Who was he to say no to a bunch of scientists?

Lucky son of a bitch.

"But it's yours anyway," I said. "You had to have got it from somewhere. Even the meteor. You got that from space."

"It's not mine." For just a moment, he looked almost distressed, but it faded away quickly. The wine probably helped. "Sorry. I didn't mean to snap at you."

"It's fine," I said. The wine was helping with that, too.

"Look," Michael said, and he grinned that way too charming grin at me. "I didn't bring you here to complain at. I brought you over for a good time. We're friends, aren't we?"

I couldn't disagree with that.

"So come on. I just bought an attachment for my boat that I know you're going to love."

***

The attachment turned out to be a parasailing rig, and he was right. I did love it. He drove me all around his lake (not really his, but since no one else wanted to handle the difficult mountain drive, it might as well have been) in his speedboat, and I got what could only be described as the best view ever.

These days I go parasailing all the time. It's really peaceful and gets my mind off everything. I only go with people I trust, though.

We were out for over an hour. Once we'd been

around the lake a couple times, Michael and I went swimming. He'd had enough people over that he had a whole stock of brand-new swimsuits ready for his guests in case of a surprise swimming party, and it was only a little creepy that he had one that would bring out my eyes.

"It's lucky you're gay," I told him as I braided my hair. "Otherwise, I'd start to think you were getting ready for a harem."

"I like to give people things," he said. "I might as well now that I have so much."

He sounded…off. It wasn't a subtle thing either. Normally, we'd have joked around about it, but now he sounded so earnest. Once again, I thought I caught some distress in his eyes before he turned away.

It stuck with me even as we played around on the beach like we were kids again. Paddleboards, water guns, diving toys with little motors so you had to chase them… Michael had it all. We even built sandcastles just close enough to the shore that the waves would knock them down as the tide came in.

It didn't come in until we'd finished the castle, though. It was pretty lucky how it worked out.

Michael looked pretty happy, like he was a kid again. I tried to keep myself smiling, but I couldn't stop thinking about how anxious he'd looked. What could he possibly have to be worried about? What was going on inside his head?

He didn't tell me. He probably wouldn't have, even if I asked. I figured it was best to just let the day keep going.

We played outside until a drone flew down and deposited a package on his dock. "Finally," Michael said, getting to his feet and dusting sand off his legs. "I thought it would never get here."

"What is it?" I asked, kicking over the last bit of sandcastle.

"Just something for you." He tossed me the package, which I started to unwrap. "I noticed your jeans got a bit wet while we were parasailing, so I figured you might want some clothes that don't smell like a lake."

They were the nicest jeans I'd ever had, and with them was a cute blouse that could have been made of satin. "When did you order these?" I asked. "You haven't been on your phone since we came out here."

"Boat computer," he said with a shrug. "What do you think? Did I get the sizes right?"

He probably had. The swimsuit fit perfectly. That wasn't what I had been thinking about, though. I'd been thinking about how the satin felt between my fingers. I hadn't been around satin since my aunt's wedding, when

I'd carefully rubbed the skirt before the ceremony. I'd never planned to actually own any, not even for my own wedding dress.

But now I had my own satin blouse, and I hadn't even had to buy it. It was a gift, bought just because, the same way I'd got people mugs or random crap from thrift stores.

But this was a satin blouse. I swallowed hard. "Thanks," I said. "I'm sure it's great."

Michael watched me anxiously. I forced myself to smile.

"I guess I'll go get dressed," I said.

He brightened at once. "I'll get lunch ready. You can use any room you like to change. Just try not to get lost."

We both laughed. Both sounded pretty strained.

***

Michael's house had a hell of a lot of rooms, so I picked one at random. It was some kind of living room, and if I hadn't been sure we were the only two people in the house, I would have felt pretty nervous about changing in it. If I hadn't known we were the only people around for probably miles, I wouldn't have done it at all, because it had floor-to-ceiling windows that let in sunlight and made everything shine. Even as it was, I felt a little nervous and changed as quickly as I could, bundling up the wet swimsuit in a soft towel he'd tossed me as we'd gone inside. I didn't even want to think of what it must be made of or how much it must have cost. Just holding it told me enough. It felt better than any other towel I'd touched.

I was pretty sure Michael had been joking when he told me not to get lost, but at least a minute passed of me just wandering and trying to find a laundry room. After another minute, I gave up on that and started hunting for a laundry floor. Another minute passed, and I would have been happy to find Michael.

Another minute. I was almost starting to think I was alone in the house.

I'd already been opening doors at random, but I gave up on each room pretty quickly once I realised it didn't have a washing machine. After a while, though, my curiosity got the best of me. Whatever the towel was made of, it was thick enough that the swimsuit wasn't leaking through it. I'd had it pressed against my stomach the whole time I was walking, and my new blouse wasn't even a bit damp. At this rate, it would hold out just about forever.

Besides, if Michael wanted to find me, he would

probably have a lot more luck than I'd had finding him. Lost people were supposed to sit tight and wait to be rescued, but it wasn't like I was wandering around a city. I was in my friend's house. I might as well poke around.

I might as well feed my own envy, because that was what wound up happening. I wandered, and I looked in rooms, and sometimes I wandered into the room. Everything I saw was stunning. Michael had giant windows that looked out over every view. Michael had an indoor pool for when it was too cold to go out on the lake. Michael had a game room with boards already set up on tables, pinned down so they wouldn't move out of the way.

I've always been a sucker for board games. I still am, really. I like some new ones, some classics…basically anything that will keep me sitting for an hour or so. The more involved, the better.

It's not much of a surprise I don't get out much. I didn't back then either.

The game room seemed as good a place as any to wait, at least for a bit, so I wandered around. Michael had just about every game that sprang to mind and plenty I hadn't even heard of. One or two I'd seen talked about online, but as something that would come out in a few months, if not further away.

"Lucky son of a bitch," I muttered, toying with a twenty-sided die. I was tempted to slip it into my pocket, but it would only be a reminder of what I'd seen and would never have. Every time I looked at it, I'd remember where it came from, and Michael would always be on my mind, even if he never asked for it back. Even if he never noticed it was gone.

Besides, the jeans were so tight it would show right through my pocket. I tossed the die idly back on the table, where it clattered for a moment before falling still.

A natural twenty. What do you know?

The table in the back corner caught my eye, and I made my way over to it. It didn't look like any of the other games; if anything, it seemed more like a roulette table, but Michael had never struck me as the gambling type. He was too steady for that.

Besides, it didn't look like any roulette table I'd seen in movies. It was red and gold, except for two sections which were both black. One had a white star that must have been made of pearl; the other was pure black, not marked by anything at all. Light poured right into it.

A little crystal ball sat in a cup by the table. I picked it up. It was heavier than it looked, but the weight felt good. It made me think the ball wanted to be thrown.

I curled my fingers around it, but before I could do

anything more, Michael called my name from the doorway. I didn't move, and he called again, louder.

He must have seen me. He must not have wanted me by the table.

His shoes tapped against the marble floor. "Hey," he said. "I've been looking all over for you. Don't you know when you're lost you're supposed to pick one place and stay there?" He grinned, but his gaze darted from me to the table and back.

"Sorry," I said, though I wasn't sorry at all. There were cracks in Michael's perfect façade, and I'd found them just by stumbling across the table.

"Do you want some lunch?" His voice was eager, almost manic. "It's just about done, and I know you'll like it. Rice flour rolls—almost as good as the ones we'd get back in college. Remember?"

I remembered dragging Michael away from campus to get *bánh cuốn* from a little Vietnamese place that everyone said was shady, but it was just surrounded by a shady neighbourhood. I remembered how nervous he'd been because until then the only Asian food he'd eaten had been Chinese takeout. I remembered we'd only ordered appetisers because back then we'd both been broke, and I guess I never told him *bánh cuốn* didn't make up a full meal.

I'd never had to. Before I got enough money to treat him to a proper dinner, he got rich.

"So, what is this?" I asked, holding up the ball. "New game no one else knows about?"

"Not quite," he said. He held out his hand, but I closed my fingers around the ball tightly. "Look, I don't know how to explain this."

"I would have thought you'd know how," I said. "It's yours, after all."

"It's not mine!" His voice echoed on the walls. "It's...I don't know."

It wasn't his. Somehow, that was enough for me. I spun the table. I rolled the ball. Michael twitched, but he didn't do anything to stop me. I'm not even sure he could have.

The ball stopped on the black section with a white star. Michael started to cry.

***

And that, as they say, is that. I still don't know what it was made me throw the ball. Probably the same thing that's about to make you throw it. I still don't even know what the roulette table is or where it came from. It showed up along with a bunch of other furniture I ordered when money suddenly started pouring into my life.

It's magic. I'm pretty sure about that. What exactly it does, I don't know, but it's got something to do with luck. When the ball landed on the star, my luck changed.

So did Michael's.

He's okay, I guess. Pretty depressed that he's lost everything. I guess I have that to look forward to, too. There's one thing I don't envy him for: he couldn't resign himself to what was coming. I've tried.

That's why I didn't hide the table anywhere. That's why I didn't stop you from picking up the ball. All of this? It's not mine. It belongs to whoever can win it.

So go ahead. Try your luck. But don't say I didn't warn you.

I have no idea what will happen if you lose.

Chasing the Digital Dragon

by Raven Corinn Carluk

My hands shook as I clenched my phone. "That cum-guzzling gutterskank." My voice cracked, further words dying in my throat. All the foul, vile, wretched curses I could never utter online choked me, begged to burst forth and find life.

I flung my phone at the couch, trying not to break it, then stomped to my kitchen and the bottle of rum waiting for me. Never talked about the drinking online—only healthy drinks and organic foods until the next trend came by. Could I be so lucky that it would be Cuba libres and chocolate?

The cap came off quickly, and I gulped spiced rum straight from the 1.75-litre bottle. Fifty mils, then fifty more. Then I broke my kiss with the alcohol. I coughed, wheezed, leaned into the burning flavour. Anger faded as a buzz kicked in. Recapping the bottle and setting it back on the counter, I felt able to focus again.

My thoughts flowed better as my skin tingled with

the rush of intoxication. I briefly wondered if I had an alcohol problem and if I was coming to rely on it. Dismissing the thought quickly, I reminded myself that being a social influencer was hard. All the top girls *had* to be doing something to keep up the façade.

It all had to be a façade, right? I couldn't be the only one using a pseudonym with a fictitious background and carefully curated posts to tell their story. No one could be so picture perfect and hashtag blessed.

Alyssa Bonner was a vegetarian, animal lover, volunteer, and deeply liberal activist. None of that was really me, yet it was everything. I always had to think how Alyssa would react. What would she say, what would she buy, what would she do? Couldn't ever let the real me peek through, lest I get a few less likes and shares.

Those little hearts meant everything to me. Same as all of us. Validating and beautiful and wonderful. Nothing matched the feeling of opening the app on my phone and seeing all the latest notifications.

How much better was it for Marissa? She was new to the social platforms, but she already had three times the following I have, with four times the interactions. Her notification screen must be so delightful.

Anger stirred again, driving me back to the bottle. It was hard enough to sculpt the persona of a social influencer without having someone leeching all my followers.

Not that my numbers had fallen, really. They just weren't growing. My posts weren't going as far, were tapering off far too quickly, but I saw Marissa everywhere. So pretty, so clever and witty, so on the cutting edge of all the trends.

At least she wasn't a trendsetter yet. Just very popular. If I couldn't crack the code, I'd never get ahead of her. And if I couldn't do that, then what would be the point of being online?

Something clattered in the basement, drawing my attention. Could he be awake already? Nothing to do but go look.

The rum may not have done much for my mood, but it certainly made my knees weak and steps unsteady. The journey down the carpeted stairs to my converted basement took more time than I expected, as I had to calculate each step before I made it. Wouldn't work to fall in front of my guest.

"Who the fuck is there?" he asked as I reached the bottom. Definitely awake. Chains rattled as he tested his bonds.

"It's okay. I'm not going to kill you." I giggled slightly as a wave of dizziness passed through me. Not the most appropriate sound when trying to reassure someone you meant them no harm.

"No, this isn't okay. Who are you?" The chains rattled again, and the chair groaned. He was wide awake and testing his strength.

Time to see if I could work a love spell while drunk.

"My name's Jennifer." I shook my head and flipped a switch. Several soft amber lights came on, creating an intimate setting in my arcane workroom. "But you should call me Alyssa. That's how everyone online knows me. And since you're going to be my boyfriend in my posts, you really should call me that." I stopped to stare at him.

He glared back, green eyes flashing against café au lait skin. Sweat caused his hair to curl tighter and his shirt to stick to his toned body. The anger he displayed told me about the passion in his heart, let me know how much stronger I'd need to make the spell.

"Jennifer. Alyssa. Doesn't fucking matter. Let me the fuck go." His voice was raspy, not quite deep enough to form an actual growl.

I shook my head, moving towards my workbench of spell components. "You're not going to want to use that kind of language if I have you start your own posts."

"The fuck?" He rattled his chains again.

"Please try to keep up," I said, glancing over my

shoulder. "It's really not that hard, sweetheart."

He said nothing, just glared with a set jaw. I smiled and wrinkled my nose at him before returning my attention to the herbs and crystal components arrayed along the velvet-covered workbench.

"I've always been one of those influencers who believes one's love life should be kept to oneself. Need to stand out on my own, as a strong and intelligent woman who doesn't need a man for validation. Some of my most favourited posts are about *just* that thing, and I wanted to keep rolling out more content like that."

"But times are changing. Seems like the followers *want* stories of love and couples and resisting as partners." I shuddered, clenching my fists on the benchtop. "Marissa is showing off her new bae, some scrawny barista, and I can't let her gain even more traction."

"So go get yourself a boyfriend. Or a girlfriend. Whatever," he swore again, and the chair creaked with his movements.

I laughed, pulling a mortar towards me. "That's what I'm doing, Dariesque."

"My name's Eric."

"No. We're going to need something more ethnic sounding."

"*Ethnic?* Bitch, just say you mean *black*."

Shaking my head as I began selecting the proper herbs. "No, my beloved, I wouldn't say that. But I know how the followers online work, what their expectations are. *They'll* expect you to have a less...*white* name. We can't let ourselves be accused of all those icky things, so Dariesque it is."

"You're really fucking crazy." Eric made a disgusted sound.

"Only because it drives a girl mad to try to keep up with the online world. Say the right thing. Post the right pictures. Repost the right people. Have the right sympathies. It's more exhausting than the most intense magical ritual I've ever performed," I chuckled, crushing herbs with my quartz pestle.

"So you do magic?" He didn't sound like he was trying too hard to get out.

"That's one way to describe it." I added charged water to the mix, whispered words of power as I stirred widdershins. "I'm from a long line of witches. Magic is in my blood, power in every breath."

"Meaning you use magic on the Internet to get what you want?"

"Oh no...no...no, my dear. That's not how that works." Alcohol and magic power swam together in the back of my skull, making me feel lighter than the air. I

closed my eyes as I completed the love spell.

"Can't cast spells on the Net," I continued as I turned to face him, mortar in hand. "It has its own language and rules and rituals. No witch can work spells online." I smiled and winked as I went to my shelf of goblets.

Eric's voice trembled with something akin to fear. Not all the way scared, but he was working his way towards being so. "What *are* you doing then?"

"Nothing much." I poured the dark liquid into a tall goblet. Its sweet scent wafted up to me as I turned to face my guest. "Just a variant on a love spell. Something to help you wear the persona of Dariesque a little better."

He struggled against his bonds, eyes widening, cheeks draining of colour. "The fuck you will. Get that away from me." Eric tried to kick, but I had chained his legs more tightly than his arms.

"Just relax," I cooed, standing by his side. "It will all be perfect soon. Just perfect." I laughed, eager to show off my bae to the stuck-up Marissa. She'd never be able to top this.

Urning Back Lost Things

by Frances Tate

The day we met, Penny McLean, my blue eyes and crown turned green. For years, I lived in the shadow of your perfection.

You graduated with a double first. Studies over, turned down a full-time modelling contract.

Didn't turn down Jamie's diamond.

I want him back. And everything else you took.

Cutting brake pipes, I watched you finally go down in flames. Stole your cremated remains.

No longer consumed by envy, I consume you.

A bone fragment lodges in my throat, leaves me choking. As darkness closes in, it occurs to me that you've come back, like a bad Pen—

Summer and the Deal

by Rhiannon Bird

Summer rubbed her arms. The rock made it hot and her skin prickled. She stood in a huge antechamber—black pillars broke out of the rock and shot into the ceiling. Beneath her feet was a carved, smooth path that wound its way to a large set of dark double doors. She didn't need to touch them for the doors to swing open. The chamber was almost as big as the last one, the black rock smoothed around the entire space. The only thing inside was a tall throne carved from the black rock itself.

Summer stepped cautiously inside. "Hello?"

Her voice bounced around and right back to her. She crept further inside—there was no movement. As she passed where the doors had opened to, they slammed shut, leaving her in darkness. She jumped around to face the doors but couldn't see a thing.

"They really aren't the main event, love," said a smooth voice.

Light began to fill the space; though it didn't seem to come from anywhere in particular, it was just enough for her to make out the now-occupied throne. The man had a dark suit on, the shirt untucked, and tie loose around his neck. He lay draped across the throne, his messy hair sticking in every direction and smiling widely at her.

"I will admit I'm impressed that you found this place. No one's been here in years."

Summer straightened and smoothed her dress. "I've heard that you grant wishes."

He chuckled and cocked his head to the side. "You've been talking to the wrong people if that's what you're looking for."

Her face fell, and he held up a finger.

"But a deal is much more my style."

"A deal," Summer spluttered. "I don't have anything to give you." She held out her empty hands to prove it.

He scrunched up his nose and jumped off the throne. "I'm not in the business of the material."

"What?" she asked as he walked closer.

He stopped and looked her up and down. "You really don't know anything when you decided to seek me out."

Summer lifted her chin. "People say you can give me what I want."

"That is true." He nodded, rubbing a hand through his hair. "An interesting case, yours. A best friend who is marrying the man you love, has the promotion you worked for, and who your parents always compare you to.”

Everything in her body tensed. “How did you know that?”

“I know a lot of things, love.” He winked. “The question is what are you willing to give me to have all that instead of her.”

Summer’s mouth pressed firmly together as she watched him.

“How about your soul?”

She raised an eyebrow. “That’s impossible.”

“What you’re asking for is impossible.” He clicked his fingers, and a staff made of gnarled wood appeared in his hand. “Do we have a deal?”

Summer opened her mouth, then thought better of it. “What do you mean, my *soul*?”

“It would just ground your soul to me, so when you die, it will come directly to me.”

She chewed on her lip—she had come this far.

He twirled the staff in his hand. “I can give you Andy, the promotion, and even your parents’ approval.”

She opened her mouth to say no. That was the right thing to do; why would this lunatic be able to do anything for her? “Done.”

“Brilliant,” he said and clicked his fingers. Two massive fires burst into existence next to the throne, turning the already hot chamber into a sauna and filling the space with intense light. Then with a flick of the staff, bits of both flames broke away and formed a circle above the throne.

"Who are you?" she breathed.

"You can call me Lucifer and I'm not going to lie, love—this is going to hurt."

Her eyes snapped to him. His wide smile was the last thing she saw before flames engulfed her vision, and she screamed as they seared her skin.

***

Summer gasped and shot up. A room came into focus. No chamber, no fire, no Lucifer. She calmed down and wiped sweat from her forehead, then pulled her hand back in surprise as something cold brushed it. Metal. A beautiful diamond ring winked up at her from her finger.

"Morning, babe."

She looked up in surprise as a shirtless Andy walked into the room, a coffee in each hand. He passed one over to her, and she could feel her head spinning. She still felt in a daze as he climbed under the covers and moved over to lean against her.

"You ready to move into the new office?"

She blinked. "What new office?"

His eyebrows furrowed. "Didn't the promotion include an office on the higher level of the firm?"

"Oh right," she said, jumping lightly as he slid an arm around her and drew her against his chest. "I don't know where my head is this morning."

He chuckled and kissed her shoulder. "Just don't forget about dinner at my mother's tonight."

"I won't forget," she said, sinking back into him; finally, she seemed to have grasped onto her bearings. Whatever the lunatic had done, it worked.

He hummed, and she felt it through her back as his chest moved. "You still have two hours until you need to be at work."

She glanced at the little red numbers on the clock that flashed back at her. Andy's lips were on her shoulder again.

"I can think of something we can do to fill in the time," he said softly, his lips moving further up onto her neck.

***

Summer balanced the box on her arm as she walked towards the elevator. She still felt flushed from this morning—never in her life had she thought Andy would look at her the way he looked at Felicity. It still gave her chills. The lift opened and she stepped inside, almost jumping in surprise. "Oh morning, Felicity."

"Morning," she said brightly. "You need any help moving up to the new office?"

Summer looked her over again. She looked fine. "No, I've got it covered." She didn't look crushed like she should have. Summer had taken over her life, and yet she seemed…happy. If that was possible. "We still on for Chinese today?"

Felicity's expression flickered for a moment. "Why would we have lunch together?"

"We spend every Wednesday lunch at the Chinese place on the corner." Summer frowned; it had been a tradition ever since their first day here together as interns.

"I'm sorry," Felicity said, frowning. "You might be confusing me with someone else. We hardly even talk."

Summer felt a lump form in her throat. "Right. Sorry, I must have plans with someone else." Her phone started ringing. It sat on top of the box she was holding, and a photo of Andy with a cheesy grin flashed up on the screen. Summer felt a flash of guilt and looked up at Felicity. "It's Andy."

Felicity nodded, giving her a quizzical look as the

doors opened for her floor and leaving Summer alone in the elevator. She didn't know who Andy was, Summer realised. She frowned; the three of them had grown up together, and yet Felicity didn't even have a spark of recognition at the name.

She hurried to her new office, dropping the box onto the desk and running a shaking hand through her hair. Trying to distract herself, she pulled out files and picture frames from the box she had just brought up. One was her degree in a beautiful black frame, her biggest achievement: making it through law school. She carefully hung it on the wall.

She deserved this promotion, Summer reassured herself.

Her eyes caught something. The degree didn't look quite right, there was something off. Summer jumped back—the University of South Australia. She blinked and ran her fingers over the words. But she had gone to Flinders University, she could still remember enrolling with Felicity. Except she didn't. Whatever place this was, she and Felicity didn't know each other.

Summer was feeling dizzy again, like the world was shifting in and out of focus as her eyes caught something else. She pulled out the picture frame: it had an older couple smiling widely at the camera. Summer sat back in her chair, staring at the faces that stirred nothing inside her—she didn't recognise them at all.

Her phone rang again, and she snatched it. On the screen was the face of the woman in the picture. Above it, the word MUM flashed repeatedly. With shaky hands, she pressed answer and put it to her ear. "Hello?"

"Hey, sweetie." A voice she didn't recognise. "I just wanted to wish you good luck today. Me and your father are so proud of your promotion."

Summer put a hand up to her mouth, trying to hold back sobs. She managed to force out a thank you.

"Can you and Andy come over for dinner tonight?"

She used her shoulder to hold the phone to ear as she pounced on her laptop. "No, we have dinner with his mum."

"Oh, that woman really gets under my skin."

Summer rolled her eyes; Mrs Davis was eccentric, but she meant well. Her mum—her real mum—had always enjoyed the weirdness. She tapped her foot as the screen loaded, then she clicked on the Facebook icon. "Look, I really have to go. How about we come over tomorrow night?"

The woman on the other end of the line laughed. "Oh Summer, you forgot that I have Bingo on Thursday nights."

Summer cringed—her mother hated bingo.

"Plus, your father has his yoga session late tomorrow."

Her father doing yoga? He wouldn't have been caught dead… "My boss is coming. I've got to go."

"Okay, love you, sweetie."

Summer hung up and threw the phone across the room, shivering. Her gaze moving back to the loaded screen. She blanched, the name that popped up beside her profile picture. Summer Jones. She whispered, "Jones." It sounded wrong. Summer spun, and sure enough, it matched the name on her degree; she hadn't even noticed it before. "Get a grip," she chastised herself and turned back to the screen. Her fingers flew across the keyboard as she typed in her mother's name: JULIA WELLS. Summer held her breath as the loading symbol popped up on the screen.

A list of Julia Wells appeared with a string of different photos, but she couldn't see her. Her eyes scanned rapidly, and she felt like throwing up—where was she?

Summer scrolled down, and she almost cried with relief. There was her Mum, smiling up at her from the tiny picture. She sank back in her chair in relief and clicked on the profile. There weren't many photos, her Mum was never that up to date with posting, but there was one with Dad there. She felt a tear slip out as she stared at them. Her parents. They were condescending and a little harsh, but they were hers. They loved her in their own weird way, and here, here, they didn't even know her. Tears slipped out and were falling down her cheek before she could stop them.

Summer's phone rang from the corner of the room and she groaned, considering just leaving it there. With a heavy heart, she walked over and picked it up. Andy smiled up at her and she smiled weakly at the screen. The tears hadn't stopped falling.

"Heads up that my Mum is going to want to give you some old creepy necklace. Dad says that it looks terrible, but once we get home, we can stuff it into some old box and only get it out when she comes over."

She tried to keep her voice even. "Yeah, sounds like a plan."

"Are you alright?" he asked, concern lacing his voice.

"Yeah, yes. I'm fine. Just feeling a little sick."

"It must be because you're up so high in your office now." He laughed.

"Yeah." She didn't have the heart to tell him she spent half her time before going to meetings on levels higher than this one. "I'll see you tonight."

"We're leaving at four, you good with that?"

"Yeah, see you then."

"Love you," he said lightly and hung up.

Summer barely made it to her trash can before she threw up. Just to be perfect timing, her boss walked in and immediately sent her home to rest.

That was worse—everything was already so out of control, and now without the distraction of work. She had torn through the house. Summer had looked through everything she could, trying to piece together what her life was now.

Felicity was nowhere, pictures of her fake parents everywhere, and it seemed that she'd only met Andy just after she graduated. That was important, no childhood stories about him.

By the time he made it home, which was half an hour after they were supposed to leave, she was pacing back and forth trying to calm herself down. This all felt like a cosmic joke. She had spent forever hating her life and wishing she had Felicity's. Had even tracked down Lucifer to get it, and now everything felt wrong. It wasn't Felicity's life; it was some twisted version of her own.

"I know I'm late," Andy said, rushing in and kissing her on the cheek. "I just need to change my shirt before we leave."

Focus on Andy, she took deep breaths, at least she had Andy. But not her best friend Andy she'd grown up with, she had Andy who she dated. That was important to remember.

"Let's go." He rushed past her to the car.

He held her hand as they drove. She forced a smile but couldn't bear to look at him. He just reminded her of the childhood she'd lost, the best friend who didn't even know her anymore. Her phone rang, and she quickly rejected the call, forcing herself not to roll her eyes.

"Why are you avoiding your mum's calls?" he asked, rubbing his thumb over her hand.

She resisted the urge to pull her hand back and sighed. "It's a long story."

As they drove, he kept glancing at her, and she could feel her teeth grinding.

"I'll tell you later, okay?"

He seemed to relax after that. They didn't say anything else as they drove the rest of the way.

Andy jumped out of the car and hugged his parents. Summer pushed herself out of the car; she just wanted this day over. Then she could try to fix it all later. Felicity, she could win over, she was sure, and being with Andy would take a little bit of an adjustment, he was the same yet different. Her parents were a problem she didn't have a solution for yet.

"Summer!" Mrs Davis exclaimed and pulled her in for a hug.

Summer smiled and relaxed into the hug. This was it, the only normal thing that had happened all day. She almost burst into tears again, struggling to force it back down. Mr Davis gave her a side hug. "How ya doing, honey?"

"It's been a long day." She sighed.

He chuckled, "It's always a long day."

Summer managed a weak smile at him before Mrs Davis grabbed her hand and pulled her into the house. Probably lucky since she couldn't bear to look at the porch that her mother and Mrs Davis had spent countless days sitting on watching their kids mucking around in the garden. "I have something for you, dear." They stopped, and she opened a drawer, rummaging through it. "I swear it was right here," she muttered.

"Come on, Mum." Andy squeezed Summer's shoulders. "You can find it after dinner."

"It's this beautiful necklace, very old and powerful." Her face was flushed with excitement.

Summer shared a small smile with Andy as he shook his head. That felt a like the old them at least. "It sounds lovely."

"Got it." Mrs Davis pulled it out from the back of the drawer and presented it to Summer. It truly was horrific. There was a giant feather, two rough squares that looked like they were made of bone, and a large piece of wood that had a symbol carved into it. As soon as she touched it, Summer wanted to throw it away. It sent shockwaves through her fingers that climbed their way up her arm. Her legs started to wobble, and she leaned back into Andy.

"Thank you so much, Mrs Davis." Her head was starting to spin as she forced out the words.

The little woman clapped happily. "It wards off evil spirits."

Summer opened her mouth to reply, but the shocks had reached her chest and she gasped, falling back into Andy.

"Summer," he called, holding her limp body. "Summer. Dad call an ambulance," he cried frantically, as Summer was pulled from her body. She was watching the scene from above. Then it was gone, and she was moving fast enough that the world became a blur. Everything felt different, wrong. She knew she wasn't herself anymore, that she was something else now.

The black rock chamber came into focus around her, though this time she was right in front of the throne.

"Hello, love." Lucifer sat in his throne and held up the necklace that Mrs Davis had given her. "Not hard to swap out the fake with something a little more potent. You shouldn't touch something that wards off evil spirits when you've made a deal with the Devil," he said, grinning.

The Greatest Show

by Lisa Fox

Pigs raced through the falling embers, their glittered tutus shimmering in the flames that licked their heels. Dancing bears waltzed, oblivious, through the centre ring. Only the tigers' roars, loud as the screams of the surrounding inferno, jarred them from their trance. Above, trapeze artists swung through the fire, their bodies a contorted death pendulum suspended above safety nets that had long since crumbled to ash.

Alfred Mollow stood in the middle of the burning circus, beaming. Scraps of flaming canvas floated around him, reflecting off his round-rimmed glasses like snowflakes in hell. Embers burned holes into his polyester grey suit; he laughed as the fabric smoked. He raised his arms as walls of fire rose, seemingly at his command.

He was the Ringmaster now.

Alfred had never meant for any of this to happen. Neither a showman nor spectator, all Alfred wanted to do was to keep the books in order. Keep a balanced ledger so the show could go on. Keep the profits flowing so his sweetheart would bat her eyes in adoration of his intelligence, maybe let him steal a kiss every now and then before she applied that rich, red rouge to her full lips before taking centre stage.

Alfred was a simple man, with simple needs. And his sonofabitch brother knew that. Robert, who was never content with having everything, needed to take the one thing that mattered most to Alfred.

And now, Robert's body lay in a smouldering heap, a muddy footprint stamped across the back of his gaudy red satin jacket. His shiny top hat lost its glimmer, crushed and burning in the dust of the circus floor. The star of the show—a sad clown trampled by the masses.

Alfred smiled. That lecherous, gluttonous bastard deserved it.

***

Layla was Alfred's girl.

Every night, the world stopped as Alfred marvelled at Layla leading the elephant parade in the grandest of all grand finales. Pachyderms pranced around the centre ring; they followed Layla as she knelt on the broad shoulders of Elbreth the Elephant. Layla was at the epicentre of the greatest show, her light a beacon for both man and beast.

How the crowds gasped and cheered, captivated by

her beauty and grace! To Alfred, she was everything. Her gaze shined upon him like the rhinestone crown that adorned her flowing blonde hair. His knees weakened each time she looked past the glitter and glitz, blowing kisses at him—plain old Alfred in his grey suit and suspenders. As she basked in the glow of the spotlight, he lurked in the shadows with a pencil behind his ear and the ledger tucked under his arm.

But it didn't matter, for in those moments, Alfred shared her stardom. His love for her was as grand as the Big Top, her laughter as rich as a calliope. He showered her with gifts—chocolates and daisies, her favourite; her palm always so soft as he laid crisp banknotes in her hand.

Their special secret. Layla deserved only the best.

Robert had mocked Alfred for his affection towards Layla. *A drooling puppy,* he called him. *A sideshow freak stalking a queen.*

But Alfred knew better. He believed in their love.

***

Robert had invited Alfred to his trailer that afternoon to review the books. It was unlike Robert to leave the door unlocked, but on this day, he'd instructed Alfred to enter when ready.

It was all a ruse.

As Alfred pushed the trailer door open, he was struck as dumb as a mime as the flash of arms and legs and flesh assaulted him. The sour stench of sweat and sex sent Alfred running, demanding answers from stars that hid beneath the mask of day.

How could she?

Always the showman, Robert had planned for Alfred to catch them *in the act*. Robert didn't love Layla—he could never love Layla the way that Alfred did. As Alfred ran, he heard Robert's chortling cut through him with a knife thrower's precision. Robert had set out to remind his brother that beauty was reserved for the beautiful. To remind Alfred that he was but a field mouse who should be grateful to feast on the droppings of elephants.

Alfred gave. Robert took.

But the circus program was about to change.

***

Layla pulled a white satin robe over her glittery costume. *It didn't mean anything. Life in the circus and all,* she'd said. She kissed him on the cheek, leaving a crimson lipstick stain. *You'll get over it.*

Alfred hadn't got over it.

All he saw was a red veil, and behind it, the showstopper—Layla with Robert, entwined in the soiled and rumpled sheets of a dimly lit trailer.

So he dragged Layla from her dressing room into the night, cross and confused, black kohl lining one eye like a shiner.

Are you insane?

His eyes red-rimmed, his jaw stone, Alfred took a swig of the moonshine he'd pilfered from the stash his brother kept behind the camel pen.

Layla had cried out for Robert then, and he ran towards them, arms flailing and coattails flying like a cape in the wind. *What are you doing?* he'd shouted.

Alfred tightened his grip on Layla's arm; his fingers dug in like spikes holding a tent. He bared his teeth in an attempted grin, looking more like a ravenous tiger than the jolly clown his brother mistook him for.

It's almost showtime.

But Alfred wasn't thinking of the children in the stands, nor the dancing animals, nor the vendors hawking popcorn and cotton candy.

Let her go, Robert had hissed. *No one needs to see such a spectacle.*

Alfred hadn't needed to see such a spectacle either.

***

The din of the gathering crowd filled the tent behind them as happy patrons took their places in the bleachers. Alfred had released Layla into Robert's waiting arms and the two had turned away from him, glowering.

Showtime.

Alfred called out to them as he lit a match and tossed it onto a hay bale. It erupted into a plume of fire. He clapped and cackled with glee as the flame inched like a spider's legs down towards the edge of the nearby tent. Smoke billowed into the August night.

Alfred, no! Layla shouted.

The camels spit and whined as the gritty cloud engulfed them. Alfred released their holding gate; they galloped forward, crashing through the canvas opening of the Big Top.

He released the pigs next, then the dancing bears, and the tigers. The air crackled around him. Fire licked at the walls of the circus tent; it charred at the ropes holding the structure and ate through it like a lit cigar.

Like the smelly El Coronas Robert chomped on every night, when the performance was done.

This was the greatest show on Earth.

The audience shrieked and stampeded under the Big

Top. Robert raced inside to quell the chaos.

Always the leading man, Alfred thought. *But no more.*

Layla screamed, pleading for him to stop. Her satin robe fell from her shoulder, her sequined costume peeked through. Firelight reflected off her skin.

Skin ruined by Robert's grubby hands.

Alfred shrugged, taking another deep swig. He threw his jug into the flames and smiled a maniacal smile as he raced towards the elephants. He released their shackles, ignoring the hot metal searing his hands and the stomping of their massive feet around him. They raised their trunks—*In protest? In triumph?*—as their voices bellowed in the night.

Layla stood before her charges, her red lips forming a perfect O, a scream held tight in her throat. Elbreth raced over her, the beast's footfalls tearing her robe, her milky white skin, into tatters, crushing her skull and leaving her body in a bloody heap in the dirt.

Life in the circus, Alfred thought. Howling with laughter, he dashed towards the burning tent, a field mouse roaring amid the silence of elephants.

The Fake

by Nicola Currie

After two hours, three hundred photos, and forty different filters, I go for selfie eighty-nine, surrounded by a cherry blossom border to emphasise my pink dress and lips.

"You're such a poser, loser," my grungy little brother says, as he passes my room on his way back from the kitchen to the computer in his bedroom, empty-caloried sustenance in hand. "What's the point? Your posts never look anything like you."

"Says the waste of space who spends his time pretending with his sad little gamer friends that he's a warrior elf or whatever the hell you're supposed to be."

"That's different, duckface. Obviously no one really believes that's who we are. We're not pretending that we aren't pretending. And at least I have real friends."

I show him the finger but he smirks as he walks away, knowing he's stung me. A cold emptiness fills my chest for a moment but then I look at my phone, lighting up and pinging with love for me, with like after like, heart after heart.

"Looking sexy, babe," ravi_the_raver says.

"OMG, I love your hair!" TheRealKittyD says.

"Marry me…" BicuriousGeorgia says.

I have thousands of followers. That counts, I tell myself. Life is online now. It's only logical that friends are too.

Still, I head to the club later than I planned, knowing that nobody is waiting for me, that nobody is wondering where I am.

A few minutes in, I see a girl dressed in a sequined jumpsuit, her hair coloured in an ombre of purple, her every movement effortlessly cool. She is everything I wish I could be. I dance nearby and casually bump into her, as my way into a conversation.

"Sorry, this place is packed!"

"No problem," she says, barely fazed, barely aware of me through the noise. "Huh?"

"I said I love your hair! Mind if I take a picture to show my hairdresser?"

The girl smiles and doesn't protest when I fling my arm around her and put my face next to hers. She even makes a peace sign with her fingers—perfect.

Photo taken, I thank her and drift away. I have no further need of her. I post the picture with #squad #clublife #bff #girlsnight. Instantly, my online profiles are busier and more alive than the club on its wildest night, and the crowd I invisibly walk through might as well have melted away.

But the evening has just begun. I spend the next few hours drifting from new friend to new friend. Some middle-aged predator in a designer suit invites me and a bunch of other girls not yet quite out of their teens to join him. He's clearly a creep, but the ten minutes he spends with his arm over my shoulders is worth it for the expensive champagne he gives me to drink and the snaps I get of it. #elite #money #luxury #princess.

When he moves to fill up the glass of the girl on his other side, I take the opportunity and slip away. Another girl quickly grabs my seat, and he moves his arm back across her shoulders now. I am not even sure he notices the switch.

Somebody else does, though. As I head for the door, I see the purple-haired girl looking at me, frowning. Time to go.

It gets a little close like that sometimes, but no one ever really notices what I am doing. Everyone is too busy with their friends, themselves, most doing something not too dissimilar to what I do. I move around all that noise, that living, that connection without being seen.

Not a bad night altogether, I think. I hold my camera

high above me as I lie in bed, eyes closed, curled up, taking and loading the picture with #goodnight. Almost 1200 likes in all this evening and sixty-five new followers. I'll take that.

Sixty-five new friends, I think, as I drift off to sleep, dreaming of sequins and champagne. I dream of the people I met too, but it's as though I become them, that I step inside, like they are all different versions of the cooler, prettier, better person I could be.

I don't check my phone straight away when I wake late the next morning. After I've loaded a full night's content, it is always a rush to see how many likes I get overnight, so I enjoy the anticipation. I take a long bath and then, finally, reach for my phone.

My heart skips a beat as I see the notifications coming in a constant stream, pinging in second after second without fail, like my phone has its own heartbeat. This is what I have been waiting for. I've tried everything I can think of to make my posts go viral. I wonder which one of them finally hit. I open the first platform and read the first notification that appears.

"Oh my god, that is so pathetic. Mortifying."

Huh?! This time my heart doesn't skip a beat. It's more like it freezes, like my blood turns cold.

"Lol, busted. Loser!"

"What an attention whore. #InstaSlut"

"This is seriously creepy. It's a form of stalking when you think about it. I'm reporting this post."

What the fuck is going on?!!!

There are so many comments coming in that I struggle to see what the issue is until I check another platform, and there it is.

The purple-haired girl.

"Who the fuck are you?" her first comment says. "BFF? More like WTF?"

"Wait…you don't even know her?" someone asks her back.

"Not at all. She said she wanted to take a picture of my hair for her hairdresser! But then I saw her taking photos of everyone all night, hopping from person to person, like she knew everyone even though she was on her own. Does anyone actually know her?"

Shit. It looks like she tagged the name of the nightclub, and that's when things exploded.

"I didn't even know she took this picture," one guy said. "I thought she was kind of weird."

"This is hilarious. Sorry, bitch, but I'd never be in your #squad. So sad."

"Fuuuuckkk…looks like she has been doing this for months. Look at her earlier posts. This is mental. It's like her whole life is fake."

My entire virtual house of cards has fallen down. I'm alone in my room, detached, and yet I feel like I'm naked in a spotlight in front of the whole world, burning with the shame of knowing I am a lesser thing than everyone else, that I am not like they are.

I can fix this. I have to. I delete every photo from the night before and the comments that appeared underneath them vanish too. I put on a little makeup—neutral tones—and tousle my hair. I take a photo of myself stretching awake and load it with #lazysundayvibes.

My plan is to act like nothing is wrong, but I instantly realise it's a bad move. The angry faces and lols come in thick and fast. My follower count is suddenly a timer that is running out as I am abandoned. My wall is soon nothing more than a growing list of insults and profanity.

"Crazy bitch!"

"Get a life. You know, one that actually belongs to you…"

"Eww, she's skanky anyway. Why would anyone follow her in the first place?"

I should have known it wouldn't be that easy. With hands shaking, I type out a post that I hope will limit the damage, trying to sound breezy, unhurt, unbroken.

"Wow! It seems my posts have sparked some debate,

so I thought I should clarify where I'm coming from. Photography is a passion of mine, and I'm drawn to the ways in which people interact with each other in different situations. If I've shared a photo of you here or on any of my platforms, it's because I think you are interesting or have a cool aesthetic that I find artistically inspiring. It's just my own little way of brightening people's day by sharing my quirky, artsy view of the world, because you are all so beautiful. #beauty #art #culture #photography"

"What utter bullshit."

"Do you want a spade so you can keep digging that hole for yourself? Such a phony."

"LMAO. Pretentious twat."

The insults still roll in, and my followers continue to abandon me. Everything starts to blur together as my eyes tear. I spent months building this online life for myself, and in less than a day, it has fallen apart. All I can do is shut off all comments. I'll hide my profiles for a while, hide away in a friendless, virtual wilderness. In a few weeks, a month maybe, I can start again. I have to start again. Why is it so easy for everyone else? I'm so alone.

The final comment that comes in as I shut things down gives me the tiniest bit of hope.

"You guys are going way over the top. Chill the fuck out on this girl! I think her photos are kind of cool."

I click on her profile to check out who she is, to make sure she isn't just another troll. She seems genuine, with a decent but not particularly impressive number of followers. She posts about tv shows she likes, photos of her dinner, social causes she believes in, charity sponsorships, and family weddings. She looks completely normal.

Everything I wish I could be.

My jealousy means a part of me hates her, but she is the only one who offers me comfort, so I make a gesture of gratitude. It's small, but it is the most genuine I have ever allowed myself to be.

I message her directly.

Hi Ella. Thank you.

I lower my screen, ready to abandon the shattered bones of my online life, when I almost drop my phone in shock. No one ever rings me, but it's her on video chat. It's Ella.

"Hi, it's Rosy May, right?" she says, effortlessly cheery in a way that makes me feel warm and jealous at the same time.

"Actually," I say, blushing, "Rosy May is just my…my…"

"Your brand name, I get it. Listen, I know it's kind of weird a complete stranger calling you directly, but I'm assuming you're not having the best morning. I couldn't live with myself if I didn't check that you were ok."

I am genuinely moved and the first part of my heart stitches itself back together.

"That is so nice of you," I answer. I don't want to come off like a complete loser, so I try to play it cool. "I'm completely fine. It's kind of funny, really. People on the Internet can be so reactionary."

She is silent for a moment, looking at me, smiling with big kind eyes. "Except you're not ok, are you? It's ok, you don't have to pretend with me. Let's be real."

I burst into tears and, as I cry for ten minutes straight, she comforts me, tells me to let it all go.

"Doesn't that feel better?" she asks, and I nod. "It's good to get it out of your system and then you can move on." She pauses for a moment, then her eyes light up with an idea. "I know! I recently signed up to these new online exercise classes where you connect with the instructor virtually on one half of the screen but can chat with and encourage other members in the class on the other half. I think the first session is free, so why not sign up and do it with me so we can continue chatting? Otherwise, I have to go, the next class is in ten minutes."

I go to the web link she sends me. *Jesus, how much?! But* like she says, the first session is free, so I sign up, planning to cancel after the first session before they automatically take like half my savings for a six-month subscription.

I move our chat over to my computer and get changed into my gym gear. She is right. I feel fantastic once the class is over, but not because of the endorphins. This is the first time in a long time I have had someone to talk to. This is the first time I have really had a friend.

"Well, it's been a blast, but I have to go meet my boyfriend. Will I see you in the next online class tomorrow?"

I'm in class the next day, and the day after that, and then every day. Talking to Ella quickly becomes the only thing I care about. I don't even look at my followers anymore and haven't posted a new photo since the fallout. What I have with Ella is so much better. It's real.

Soon, she is so much more than just an exercise buddy. My whole world starts to open up as I become more like her. She lives a few hundred miles away so we haven't met up yet, but she knows my city well. She recommends the best restaurants nearby and bands I should go see. I am even reading for, like, the first time ever, as she suggests books I should buy so we can talk about them. I do it all, and in a few weeks, I'm messaging or video chatting with her a dozen times a day. She always answers and always has something new to talk about.

The only problem is the amount of money it is costing me.

It's not that I mind. Ella is everything, I don't care how expensive it is—going to all the places she suggests, buying clothes she says are my style, joining in with the subscriptions she has. But I don't have it. I blow through the money I have been saving for university in less than a month.

But it's Ella. I can be real with her. I'll explain.

"That sounds like an amazing suggestion, Els, but things are a little tight. Maybe there are some free eBooks we can read together and talk about instead?"

I immediately feel awful when Ella looks crushed.

"I had no idea you were struggling," Ella says. "I feel awful. Just when I thought we might have the chance to meet in person too."

What?! My heart races with excitement. Meeting Ella, my real friend, in real life, would be everything.

"That would be amazing!" I say. "Of course, we should meet."

But Ella still looks upset. "I don't see how. I wanted to go see that musical everyone's been talking about. You know, the one we both bought the album for? It's playing at a theatre pretty much at the middle point between your city and mine. But it's like £75 a ticket and then there is the train…I mean if you can't afford it…and I was really looking forward to finally meeting you." A single tear rolls down Ella's cheek.

I don't care how much it costs. I have to get to Ella somehow. I backtrack and tell her I will figure something out. She instantly brightens and tells me to get in touch when I've sorted it.

I hang up and already know what to do.

My little brother is in his disgusting bedroom, gaming as usual. He doesn't even take his eyes off the screen as I enter.

"What do you want?" he says, blasting gunfire in his imaginary world.

I get straight to the point.

"Do you have any money? I know you're saving for that console that comes out soon. Could you lend me £100, just for a few weeks?"

He scoffs, "Why would I lend you money? Besides, why have you been buying so much random crap recently if you can't afford it?"

"It's not random crap. My friend Ella has amazing taste and has been introducing me to new stuff, that's all."

My brother laughs. "You are such a moron. You know she probably isn't real, right?"

A coldness runs down my spine. "What the fuck do you mean not real?"

My brother pauses his game and turns to me, rolling his eyes. He grabs his laptop.

"I mean not real as in fake. As in deep fake? How have you not heard of this?"

He opens his laptop and brings up an article.

Has online advertising gone too far? The deep fake friend…who doesn't exist.

"What does it mean by doesn't exist? Like, she's an actress?"

"No," my brother says, closing his computer and standing to set it aside. "As in, she's computer-generated artificial intelligence. Her face, her whole appearance, her whole personality, all created based on your data to produce the perfect friend whose only purpose is to sell you shit."

"I don't believe you. That's not Ella. I know Ella."

My brother scoffs again, "Well, the article said people who were lonely and of lower intelligence were most at risk, and let's be honest, you—"

I don't mean to hit him so hard. I don't even think about it at all actually until after I snatch the laptop from his hands and slam it across his face. It is like I jump in time from the moment I come into his bedroom to the moment he lies silently on the floor, his neck broken from the way he smashes against his desk as he falls.

I know there is only one person who can help me.

I tell her everything, tears running down my cheeks, hyperventilating, desperate, no longer knowing how I can live.

She looks at me silently for a few seconds, with a fixed smile, with unseeing eyes, like she is struggling to compute everything, like she has no reaction available for this situation. Finally, she finds something, and she speaks to me with her usual sunny tone.

"I can help with that. There is this really dignified euthanasia clinic that has opened up just fifty miles away from you. For just £199..."

Sacrilege

by Kaitlyn Lynch

The candles were fragrant carcasses, skeletal sentinels, dozens of their little bodies scattered around the room. They laid stumpy and burnt out, smoke rising to the heavens. Burnt offerings to some old god with no name. The floor was spread with carpets overlapping—some of them were now old and threadbare, but put all together, it was a soft enough resting place. Woven designs pressed one into another in a smothering embrace, promising completeness but offering only excess instead. The whole room was one big too-luxurious shadowed altar, incensed and sacred. Watchers in the walls could tell tales of bodies coming together in muffled worship, too jealous of the tight caress of clothing on skin to allow even it to remain for very long when hands would suffice just as well.

But now it was silent. Quiet and dark.

And in the middle of it all, she sat with his head on her lap, her long fingers combing through his hair over and over again, feeling the silken texture of dark locks turn slick against her skin. He hadn't stirred in some time. Laid now with closed eyes, still body. She was content to feel his weight against her until the cosmos burst into flames around them.

The adoration was more solemn now. Their passion still hung thick in the air around them, intertwining fingers with the soot from the candles, but the craving of it was austere. Reverent. A quiet prayer passed from one tongue to another and then swallowed like communion wine. It burned just as much.

"We belong to each other," she murmured, leaning to press a tender kiss to his lined forehead. "I'll keep you safe." Hands slid down, down, down. Feeling the texture of stubbled jaw, hirsute chest under the unbuttoned top of his shirt. Flexed her fingers against the fabric there, eyes looking out into the darkness surrounding them. "I'll keep you safe."

Still, he did not respond to her touch. His body beneath her was an empty chapel at midnight; cold stone, beautiful marble. Something that was decidedly holy when the moonlight caught it at just the right angle. But hard, unfeeling. Unresponsive. If you looked wrong, it only reminded you how alone you truly are.

A single tear crept from one eye, rolled down her cheek, fell to his chest as she leaned over him. Her face turned back towards his, and she began to stroke at his face with a trembling kind of furore. The skin, delicately wrinkled, pulled and contorted under her fingers, and the tears poured more freely as she watched—watched and *felt*.

"I love you," she whispered. "I'll always love you."

Every cell in her body cried out at him, screaming for him to say something back, to take her in his arms and tell her that he loved her too, that everything would be alright and he would never leave her.

Slowly, she slipped out from beneath the heaviness of him, lowering his limp head to the carpeting and unbending numb legs to stand. He did not move. Did not speak. Did not open his eyes.

She longed for the warm, honey-thick rumble of his voice singing psalms of love, of praise, but he could no longer tell her what he felt for her. Lowering herself back to the floor, she knelt at his left side and reached for his hand. On his ring finger rested the blameful indication of their sin, the reminder that this place was not their Garden of Eden, but their own personal Inferno. Four walls where he could promise her beautiful things in the dark, whisper the sweetest words against her skin when no one else could hear, reach his bare hand into her ribcage and clutch at her beating heart…

And then go home, and another woman could feel his warm breath against her flesh and hear his heart beating and call him *hers and hers alone.*

It was almost blasphemous to destroy something as beautiful as her lover—the man lying dead in the padded dark of the living room. Perhaps it was a life for a life, though. And he made an exquisite corpse.

To love, she thought, crouched down next to him, reflecting on the gentle lines and angles of his unmoving face, is to possess. To destroy. You cannot have one without the other. Maybe he had stolen the innocence out of her love when he laid his uncovered skin on her heart, and this was the equal and opposite reaction. She was only a girl when she fell in love with him, virtuous and guileless. He had smiled at her and asked how it could possibly be a sin to love. Now, he had his answer. Was this a sin? Or was the keen, envious awareness that she lay decidedly at the outskirts of his life while he put another love firmly in the centre of his, *her* equal and opposite reaction?

Delicately, she removed his wedding ring, closing her palm around it until the metal bit into her skin.

Just like that, it was gone. No more.

Now he would be with her forever. Her and no one else. Lying on the pile of carpets in her living room— dark, with the curtains drawn—forever and a day, and no one would be any wiser. His lips were still soft, even

though they were still cold.

The old gods would answer to her now. She would decide when, and if, to ever accept this atonement from him as enough.

Yes, forever would certainly be a good start.

Heart of a Hawk

by Nikkita Bell

No one truly knew how long it had been since the usurper cast his curse.

Ticking clocks fell silent. The sun refused to set. Metal no longer rusted. Dust would not settle. And humans aged no more.

The fallen kingdom of Adelheim was a relic frozen in time.

Beneath the steam-powered city, the dark and cavernous depths of an underground refuge boomed with the worried voices of the forsaken. What was once a dank sewer had now turned into a sanctuary for those who opposed the usurper and his utopian regime. Whether rich or poor, the people bound together to escape a common evil.

And their future laid in the hands of a twelve-year-old girl.

Flame-lit torches lined the stoned walls as the stench of mildew and wet rock permeated the air. Catharina Reinhardt addressed a disoriented huddle of widows, orphans, and wounded warriors. She surveyed her people, noting their faces, familiar and new. Her attention towards their usual concerns faded as an ethereal woman stood out amongst the crowd, its spectral form unmoving. Catharina's eyes were glued to the apparition, wondering if anyone else noticed its presence.

"How can we expect a twelve-year-old girl to lead us?" cried a brittle voice.

Catharina blinked with a shiver, trying to erase the familiar woman from her view. She focused on the people, their eyes dark filled with despair, and cleared her throat.

"Sigmund Reinhardt trained me to become the leader of the Brass Hawk Society since birth," she said matter-of-factly. "He died fighting for his beliefs and left his position and people to me, his daughter. I may be young, but I'm also the only one here who knows the ins and outs of this organisation, from its secrets to its security."

The orphaned children looked to her with wide, hopeful eyes. The adults were not so easily convinced.

She continued her campaign. "I've rescued others who don't follow this new leader. We're safer together."

The crowd began to roar their outrage.

"How are we supposed to survive in a world where time no longer exists?"

"What do we do when our food supply runs out? Our farms no longer grow, our livestock cannot reproduce!"

Their shouts of anguish were lost to Catharina's ears as she again locked eyes with the spectre. There it was, staring her down in all its beauty and grace—an exact likeness of the woman she'd grown to resent: Miss Iva.

"Not again," she whispered to herself, shutting her eyes. "You're not here. You're not real."

Miss Iva disappeared when the usurper of the Adelheim throne murdered the monarchs and cast his evil time-freezing spell upon the kingdom. She was a beacon of hope, a mother figure to the children who fell victim to orphanhood. Taken by her thick golden curls and warm grey eyes, Catharina was once attached to Iva and hoped someday to be as loved and respected as she. Until she abandoned them all during their time of need. The mere memory of the woman caused her cheeks to flush and stomach to churn.

"She's a child!" a wounded soldier called out, hushing the others. "She doesn't have the stomach to lead us."

"If only Iva were still here," spoke a sullen widow. "She was so good with the children. I simply don't feel comfortable putting my faith in a girl who is younger than my son!"

"Nor old enough to kiss him, for that matter," quipped another woman.

Catharina's heart pounded as her skin flushed in

frustration. She covered her ears, grieving as their words tore through her already fragile ego. With flared nostrils and tearing eyes, she pushed through the horde of adults and disappeared into the darkness of their underground sanctuary.

***

She slammed the door of her father's study, pressing her panting body against it. The voices of the distressed survivors haunted her, shouting that she would never be accepted as their leader. The screech of a hawk startled her nagging thoughts.

"Siggi." She exhaled.

Perched upon a twisted wooden pedestal was her pet hawk, the one creature who would never judge her by her size, age, or experience. She extended her arm, beckoning her pet forward. She flew to her immediately, landing on her gloved hand and picking at her hair gently.

"They were awful, Siggi. You should have heard them."

The grand avian chittered, digging her beak under her wing. Catharina slumped to the ground and held the bird close. Siggi was gifted to her by her father before she had even hatched. She'd imprinted on Catharina the moment she emerged from her eggshell. The hawk was the sigil of the secret society her father founded for the less fortunate, the forsaken citizens of Adelheim who could not fend for themselves. He'd always planned for his daughter and her glorious bird of prey to lead the Brass Hawk Society to refuge and prosperity once he was gone.

She just hadn't expected it to happen so soon, especially while under a dark curse, a curse that forced her to live in perpetual adolescence.

"I saw Iva again today," she muttered to her pet. "Why won't she just go away? She bossed me around enough before she left us."

The spectre began haunting her the day Iva disappeared. Through every trial and tribulation, the ghost appeared, taunting her with its otherworldly presence. Siggi nuzzled her beak against her owner's cheek. Catharina caressed Siggi's spotted feathers with her knuckles.

"One of the adults at the summit said they wished Iva were still here. She said she wouldn't trust someone as young as me to lead them. One even commented that I wasn't even old enough to kiss a boy."

The hawk screeched once more.

"I can be just like her if they gave me the chance. It isn't fair. I've done everything I can to win these people over. I've given them a place to hide. I've set up rations. I even brought home an alchemist that will help secure the sanctuary. All *she* did was care for orphans. *I* was the one who kept their spirits up after their parents perished. Yet because I don't have the years or the figure of an adult, I am cast aside, disregarded… What did she have that I don't have?"

Siggi pecked at her tattered dress and worn-out leather boots.

Catharina's brow knotted in confusion, gently batting the bird's beak away from her clothes. "Grown-up clothes? She *did* always wear those pretty dresses. They made her look so beautiful. She had not one, but two men courting her at the same time. Remember? The Prince and the Commander?" She sighed, eyes glum and dark. "I've practically aged decades after what I've been through. Yet even now I dream of finding love like theirs. Pathetic, right? I'm invisible to men in *this* body."

A gust of cold wind swept through her hair and sent a chill down her spine. The girl and her pet looked up and met a luminous, silvery gaze of a haunting sort.

Miss Iva's spectre.

It beckoned the girl closer with its translucent finger. With a groan, Catharina reluctantly rose to her feet and placed Siggi on her wooden perch. Even in supposed death, the caretaker *still* managed to order her around. With heavy feet, she followed the apparition as it disappeared past the walls of the study and glided down dark hallways. It stopped at the end of the corridor before a door Catharina recognised as the entrance to Iva's private chambers. In a flash, the spectre vanished from her sight.

The desolate confines of a lady's boudoir came into view when she peeked her head beyond the door. She shielded her vision as harsh rays from the sun nearly blinded her. When her eyes adjusted to their surroundings, she studied the forgotten parlour.

An oak wardrobe caught her eye first. It was open, wooden doors revealing a collection of dresses, bodices, and skirts. Her hands roamed over each garment and stroked soft rows of silk and velvet. Shimmers of metallic gold and silver threads wove throughout each piece, shining like precious treasure hidden within a forest of fabric. She sighed deeply, desperately wishing she owned any article of clothing crafted so delicately, so flawless.

A mannequin donning an arctic blue corset stood out in the corner of the boudoir; it was hemmed with ivory lace and bound taut against its figure. She remembered this piece well; Iva was a vision of elegance the night she invited the Prince and Commander of Adelheim to join her in her private chambers. Intrigued by the secrecy of their dalliance, the little girl spent most of that night outside the door, listening to their honeyed promises of happily ever after.

By quick and erratic impulse, she began unlacing the back.

"Getting fit for your first corset is a rite of passage for any blooming woman," Miss Iva always told her.

She recalled the nights where she would watch the young woman prepare for her gentlemen callers, longing for the day when she, too, could fill the curves of an intricate bodice.

Catharina glanced at her reflection as she held the corset to her chest. She braced herself, eager to feel it snug against her thin frame, hopeful that it would reveal the curves she so desperately craved.

She wrapped the corset around her body…

And choked back her tears.

She scowled at her reflection, disgusted by her lack of femininity. She damned the usurper and his time-freezing curse, for he had robbed her of her basic biological rites; her youthful body would never swell with the gifts of womanhood. With gritted teeth and balled fists, she threw the corset on the ground.

Catharina continued her inspection, running her fingers across the polished wood of Miss Iva's vanity set.

It had remained untouched since the woman's disappearance, with an overturned silver hand mirror and hairbrush, and used lipstick among various scented oils, perfumes, and jewellery. Golden strands of hair were tangled within the bristles of the brush. She lifted a small vial of oil to her nose as she unscrewed its cap and inhaled the sweet scent.

German wildflowers.

A memory of an unforgettable woman.

She took the perfume bottles and sprayed their contents in the air. Each scent melded with the other, overwhelming her senses and filling her lungs like a thick, saccharine cloud. With a coughing fit, she dropped the glass bottle she was holding on the vanity and spilt its contents over the aged wood.

With a quiet gasp, she fell to her knees, cupping her hands beneath the edges of the vanity. The liquid coated her gloves, stinging her nose with the now bitter scent. She would be in so much trouble if she were caught playing with Iva's things. Fortunately, no one was around to care. Catharina smirked with a bitter laugh.

Underneath the vanity, dozens of shoeboxes were stacked and hidden. Quickly discarding her gloves, she grabbed the top box and looked inside. A stunning pair of golden high heels glittered before her.

"Wearing your first pair of heels is just as crucial when you transition into womanhood."

There it was again. That eerie voice in her head. The voice of Iva taunting her, a reminder that she will never afford such luxuries. Not so long as she was cursed.

Her jaw tightened.

She shoved the shoebox back, accidentally knocking the others down. One box spilt over the floor, revealing envelopes addressed to Iva. Curiosity plagued her adolescent heart as she reached for the letters and began sifting through each secret.

My dearest Iva,

I lived my life by the orders of others and whispers of fools. I had merely been existing, surviving day-to-day and dreaming of a life worthwhile. The moment you accepted my love, I knew I was no longer just existing; I was living. Thank you for being the sunshine my life so desperately needed.

Yours always,

Jenryk

Love letters from the Prince of Adelheim.

Her blood boiled as she clutched the note. She swallowed hard, forcing the bile down her throat as tears welled in her eyes. How could she ever compete for the love of *anyone* in a body so young, so underdeveloped? Are age and beauty such pivotal factors for a man's lust? If only one could give her a chance, to see her for the woman she will become rather than the immortal youth she was cursed to remain.

She wiped away her tears, her expression grim, pining over a romance she would never receive. With a darkened heart, she lamented over a life she would never have.

She would never fit into the proper attire of a lady. Never be the light of someone's life. She would never grow to be as beautiful or desired as Iva.

The young girl lifted herself from the ground, the weight of the world atop her shoulders, and carried herself to Iva's empty bed. She tucked herself underneath a blanket of furs, cocooning herself in the scent of a woman long lost—a scent she wished was her own. In her hands, the love letters of the Prince.

And soon, the little girl began to dream.

***

They'll never want you the way they want me, little girl.

The ethereal voice crept into Catharina's mind, lost in the world of her unconscious. A cold, green mist filled the expanse of her dream, clouding her vision. She was alone, without her hawk, and desperately searching for the source of such provoking words.

Come see, little girl. Come see how they fawn over me.

A small, stone cottage came into view amidst the green fog; in a flash, she found herself outside the cottage, rattling a jammed doorknob. Try as she might, she could not get inside.

Her laboured breaths echoed throughout her hellish nightmare; the voice continued to beckon her to come see, to come watch. She sprinted around the grounds, grunting in frustration as every window was too high for her undeveloped reach. She tiptoed upward, holding onto the ledge of the sill as she watched three dark, otherworldly figures cavorting in a candle-lit room. She gasped quietly as she recognised them: the handsome Prince of Adelheim, his brave Commander, and the beautiful Iva.

Can you see? They're powerless against my feminine wiles. The voice grew sadistic, as if running a dagger deep into her chest.

She'd seen this scene before when she'd spied on the trio before Iva's demise; the shadow of the Prince caressed his lips against Iva's bare shoulder while the Commander's hands gripped her hips. They moved together like a dark ballet, twisting and rotating in a lustful haze. She tensed, a heaviness forming in the pit of her stomach. Oh, if only she were older, if only she were like Iva…

How could any man ever fall in love with you? A little girl who can't even fill a bodice with that prepubescent figure.

"Stop," Catharina cried as she shut her eyes and covered her ears. With a thunderclap, her tearful eyes were forced open. She was forced to watch as not one, but two men loved the woman she craved to be.

Come now, little hawk. Watch as I live the life you'll only dare to dream of.

Her resolve had failed her; unholy curls of smoke circled around her, suffocating her into submission and weakening her knees. Tears welled in her eyes as they remained glued to the dancing shadows beyond stone walls. With an outstretched hand trapped against a frosted window, she remained forsaken. Forever forced to watch others thrive in what she so deeply craved. Forever on the outside looking in.

Forever a pathetic child.

***

Catharina awoke, gasping for air as tears flowed down her sullen cheeks. Bound by Iva's fur blanket, she fell off the bed and onto the cold floor. Her eyes fell upon the letter in her hands. The Prince's immaculate penmanship appeared against the crinkled paper, reminding her of the nightmare she nearly escaped. Visions and whispers plagued her mind, teasing her like impertinent children—like the doubtful refugees of the Brass Hawk Society. Her eyes fluttered as the romantic words sealed in ink twisted and changed. The ink turned green, nearly popping off the parchment.

You will never be like Iva.

The girl's body trembled; with an ear-splitting wail, tattered parchment rained around her.

She'd torn the letter to shreds.

Her envy and hatred for the lost woman consumed her; she grabbed the box of letters beneath the vanity and ripped through every note, destroying precious memorabilia.

And with them, the memory of Miss Iva.

In an envious rage, Catharina tore through the boudoir; she grasped the silver hairbrush and hurled it at the vanity, ripped each skirt and dress off their hangers, and threw every perfume bottle onto the floor. Shattered glass and splatters of amber liquid sullied her boots. With every ounce of strength bottled in her tiny body, she desecrated the honour of a woman craved by many and loved by all.

And there she stood, panting—a broken youth simmering in petulant fury.

A flicker of light caught her tear-soaked eye. Amidst the chaos triggered by a child driven mad with envy, a cracked mirror stood against the vanity. She squinted at her reflection and wiped away her tears. Catharina Reinhardt stormed out of the boudoir, leaving behind the destruction caused by childlike petulance. At that moment, the green heart of a little hawk turned blue; from that point on, she accepted the fact that she would never truly mature. Never grow to become a nurturer among the lost. Never grow old enough to know the love of a man. She would forever bear the burden of a child under the scrutiny of her elders, battling for their acceptance.

Forever cursed to live as a never-ageing adolescent girl.

The Throne

by R.S. Nevil

Jealousy swept over her like a coat, covering her so completely that she had a hard time controlling the rage that went along with it.

She stared at Markel, the ancient being sitting upon his throne, a beautiful blonde-headed woman sitting on his lap.

It was not the woman that she was envious of, though. Quite the opposite. She was envious of the man, envious of Markel and all that he controlled.

She wanted it for herself. Every bit of it. From the woman who sat on his lap, to the throne in which he sat. She wanted it all. His empire. His business. The women. Everything.

She continued to stare as she strode forward, quelling the rage that came whenever she saw the pompous, arrogant man.

He smiled as she approached, his fangs gleaming in the dimly lit room.

"Elizabeth, my dear. How did things go in Buffalo?"

Elizabeth rankled at the sound of his voice, irritated

by the sound of her name on his lips.

"Things went as planned," she said. "As they always do."

It was becoming harder and harder to keep the anger out of her tone, to keep the irritation from creeping through. Still, the timing was not right. She needed to wait just a little longer, and Markel would never know what hit him.

"So, I take it you had no trouble getting our shipment in?"

Markel's words brought her back to the present, forcing her to think about the question at hand.

The drugs, the same ones that she had just smuggled into the country. They were but one of the man's many avenues of revenue, one of the many disreputable businesses that he owned.

Elizabeth shook her head.

"We pay our people well to look the other way," she said. "And if they know what is good for them, they will continue to do so."

He narrowed his gaze, those orange eyes lingering a little longer than needed.

"And I assume they know the consequences of betrayal?"

This time she nodded, her head bobbing up and down

as she kept her gaze glued to him.

"They know what will happen if they mess up," she said. "They know who they are dealing with."

"And who exactly is that?"

The sound of his voice was cold, calculating; the scrutiny of his gaze held firmly upon her.

They dealt with her. She was the one that brokered each deal. She was the one who dealt with their associates across the border.

She knew better than to say those words though, knew better to voice that opinion.

"You," she said. "They know that they are dealing with you, Markel. They would not dare cross you."

Markel smiled, a sinister look lighting those eerie orange eyes.

"Leave us."

His words surprised her, a ripple of shock passing through her. They were not meant for her, though.

The blonde-headed woman rose, sneering at Elizabeth as she passed. Likewise, the few bodyguards that Markel kept around followed behind her, each of them eyeing Elizabeth as they left.

Elizabeth's blood froze, her heart stopping.

This was not good. It was never good when Markel Fazzinni did not want an audience. It meant he had something that he did not want anyone to know. And most of the time, it involved the person he had singled out.

Markel waited until the room was clear before he spoke again.

"I've been hearing rumours, Elizabeth," he said, rising from his chair. The same chair that she had longed to sit upon. That had been only moments before. And yet, those thoughts seemed a lifetime ago as Markel started towards her.

"They tell me that one of my people has been spreading lies," Markel said. "That someone in my inner circle has been sowing seeds of discontent."

He paused beside her, glancing at her even as she kept her gaze locked on the throne.

"I'm going to ask you this one time," he said. He moved, striding forward as he circled her, coming up on the other side. "Are you the one who has been spreading these seeds? Are you the one who has been spreading these rumours?"

Elizabeth took a swift intake of air, her gaze at last turning towards her master. She stared into those evil orange eyes, meeting his stare with one of her own. He was her maker, her creator, the blood flowing through her veins, now his own. He was the reason that she now lived as an immortal, that she now feed off human blood and was capable of moving faster than any human ever could.

And yet, somewhere along the way, he had lost himself. He was no longer the dark, cruel man that she had met in the early part of the century. He had softened. He had lost his way. And he was no longer fit to lead this empire. He was no longer fit to call himself part of the Ruling Council. Not when she was the one who did his dirty work.

"No," she said. "I am not the one who has been spreading those rumours. I would never betray you in such a way, Markel."

She held his gaze, staring into his eyes as the man smiled.

"Thank you," he said.

Without another word, he turned, his stride casual as he walked back towards his chair. Confusion swept over her, the uncertainty of the moment messing with her head. Was that it? Was that the entire purpose of this conversation?

Elizabeth breathed a small sigh of relief.

The fool.

She had been right. Markel was weak. He had changed over the last century. And now, he was no longer fit to rule the metropolis of New York. He deserved to die.

Elizabeth moved to attack, moved to end it all. And

stopped, the lights around her going dark, the entire room encased in a blanket of shadows.

What…?

She never got the chance to finish that thought as something hard hit her in the chest, the world tilting around her as she flew through the air. She had just enough time to catch herself, stopping herself before she slammed against the wall. It was not enough, though. Markel was on her before she could move, his fist pounding against her jaw, her words, her excuse lodged in her throat as she fell to the ground.

He was not done yet though, striking her again and again, repeated blows to her head, her chest, her body.

Pain tore through her like tidal waves, each wave bigger than the last. She tried to move, tried to escape, but she was too hurt, too abused. She could not move, could not breathe. Every intake of air eliciting an entirely new wave of pain.

And then, just as quickly as it had begun, it stopped. The beating. The pain. It all disappeared.

Only silence ensued. The quiet of the room broken only by the sound of her own breathing, by the sound of her wet, ragged gasps, of her lungs begging for air as she tried to understand what had just happened.

All of that vanished in an instant, Markel's rough

hand grabbing her by the head, pulling her up so that he was in her ear.

The cruel man laughed, his breath warm against her neck as he spoke.

"You are a liar," he said. "And not a particularly good one."

Panic swept through her as she felt his fangs brush against her neck. A threat. That if she so much as moved, he would rip her throat out.

"You don't think I see it?" he growled. "The way you look at that chair? The hatred in your eyes as your gaze falls upon me?"

His hands were around her throat before she could react, choking the life from her, killing her softly as he squeezed. This was it. This was how she died.

Without warning, he let go, slinging her back to the ground, her face slamming against the stoned floor as pain shot up through her spine.

"I ought to kill you," the vampire snarled. She could feel his hands on her face now, his fingers as he grabbed a hold of the inside of her cheek, pinching it, pulling her back towards him. Pain like she had never felt before radiated through her face, her eyes watering as the tears began to fall.

"But I don't think that I will."

He grabbed her by the jaw, pulling her forward until she could see the orange in his eyes. She wanted to scream. She wanted to run, to get away as fast as she could. She could not move though. She sat frozen in place, fear and panic spreading through every inch of her body.

Markel shoved something into her mouth, forcing her jaw shut as he made her swallow. Once she had, he did it again, forcing her to swallow the object for a second time.

"Those are a pair of ancient magical stones," he said. "They are filled with enough power to make even the Vampire King beg for his life."

He let go of her, her body betraying her as she whimpered, falling hard against the stones beneath her. She could still hear the sound of Markel's footsteps though, still hear the sound of the cruel man as he walked away, stalking back to his chair.

"Every time you look at this chair," he said. "Every time your jealousy and greed get the better of you, the stones will shower you in pain."

Elizabeth picked her head up, her gaze following the sound of his voice. She found him sitting in his chair, the same chair that he had just punished her with.

A scream escaped her as pain swept through her, black spots dancing in her vision as she struggled to stay conscious. Her gut boiled. Her head swam. She had simply looked at the chair. She had simply cast her gaze upon it, and the stones had acted.

Feelings of anger—of hatred—swam inside her. How could he do this…?

She never finished that thought as the pain struck again, harder this time. More excruciating. She could not help herself as she cried out, begging for it to stop, begging for the pain to go away.

It did not, though. It still lingered. A constant reminder of what would happen every time she gazed at him. Her master.

"You will live," he said. "You will live to serve me."

She whimpered at the very thought of being around this man, of experiencing the pain of looking at him day after day, hour after hour.

"You see, Elizabeth," he said. "I am not weak. I am more powerful than ever. I have not lost my way. I have only reformed it."

Her words. The same words she had spoken so often, to so many of his people.

She had been the fool. She had been a complete and utter fool.

"You see," he said. "We no longer live in the world of the Industrial Age. We can no longer bully and push our way to get what we want. No. We have to be smarter these days. More cunning. And you, my dear, have proven that you are neither."

Pain shot through her as her mind twisted on her words, her thoughts forming into a single hot jolt of pain that radiated through her. She cried out again, begging for it to stop, begging for the pain to go away.

She hated herself for it. She hated herself for being so weak, for sounding so weak. She could not help it. Every thought, every memory of her jealousy wrapped her in pain, that pain only serving to produce even more. A vicious cycle destined to repeat itself.

"Your jealousy will be your undoing," he said. "You could have gone without this. You could have made it without this. But you wanted more. You wanted to rule all of this. Even when you were not fit to. And now, dear Elizabeth, your jealousy will be your downfall."

Two rough sets of hands grabbed her, hauling her to her feet as they marched her out of the room. She had been so out of it, that she had not heard them come in. She had not heard them approach.

As they escorted her to the upper levels of the compound, she knew that he was right. She had been foolish not to see it before. Blinded by her envy, she had never seen what had been right in front of her all along.

Markel had not lost his vile and cruel nature. He had only hidden it. He had become smarter, more cunning. And she had failed to see it.

Tears began to stream down her face as the guards wrapped the cuffs around her wrists, hoisting her up so that her hands would hold her in place. She did not dare look up though, did not dare cast her gaze in the direction that she now faced. Because she knew…that through that tinted, one-sided mirror, she knew what she would see, and she knew just how much pain it would cause her.

She was stuck here, staring out over the room that she had just come from, forced to stare at that chair and her master day after day, hour after hour, for the rest of eternity.

Glass Eyes

by Ximena Escobar

Lost in the imprint of an empty white sky, Orla longed to be elsewhere. Having come to know what it's like to look into a real man's eyes, having been seen as a real woman, and having discovered that love exists just as strongly in the hearts of simple people, she didn't long for the familiar palace-bubble new circumstances had burst, but for the noise and stir the war had brought to her sights: a glimpse into the "real world," however horrific, which she and Leticia would have otherwise never even begun to fathom. Yet, here she was, more isolated than ever— far too much like a princess in a tower. Caressing the memory of a young soldier's hand, as she played with the edge of the curtain…the roughness around his fingers, his bulging beautiful vein, no longer carrying the light in those eyes—*Unforgettable eyes*—but something was wearing thin.

"It's time," said the Empress.

Orla turned, watching the tablecloth undulate like the hems of their ballgowns used to do on the palace floors, as Leticia removed a leather case under the lamp table.

Scurrying with it towards their mother, her younger sister knelt and opened the latches, lighting up with pride as a gleam beamed out through the lid; it had been her idea to sew their jewellery to their corsets.

Her bright blue eyes, however, struck Orla as especially vacant, much like the gems attached to the silk—or the empty palace, which the Resistance had surely stripped of all their paintings and history. Eerily unseeing eyes like a doll's—even for Leticia, who, having experienced the same displays of courage and love and plain intelligence as Orla had during their efforts as nurses, still considered herself to be above the people. A shining gem, never able to see beyond her own radiance.

Lifting one of the heavily studded undergarments, Leticia stretched her arms to better admire it. "It's so beautiful I should wear it for a ball," she said.

"Extraordinary things happen to extraordinary people," sighed the Empress.

I don't want to be extraordinary, thought Orla.

She gripped the windowpane, flowed into the memory of the overcast sky. She imagined the misty sight of the English shore and saw herself disappearing in a murmur of iron and steam. Susan, Lily, Daisy. Daisy was the perfect name to adopt in America, her final destination. There she would come to know the hardships where true glory is made—a love closer to dirt and earth, a closeness to the nature of being alive.

The freedom to be ordinary.

"It's time," said Leticia.

Any minute now, father would return with the convoy. Orla had always known Michail was on their side—the look he gave her as he stood in the dining room like a statue, the day he let them know about the ship. He'd whispered his name to Leticia a few days earlier, when she blatantly asked him, fluttering her doll eyelashes. They were still allowed a daily walk outside then; he'd only escorted them a couple of times but his presence, how he carried himself, was enough for Orla to sense he was one of the good ones (and Orla telling her, enough for Leticia to dare ask him his name). Leticia, unafraid to be caught and reprimanded. Unafraid for his safety—something which didn't even cross her mind— the trouble she'd get him into were he to be discovered showing the slightest notion of loyalty or liking towards them.

Michail and the dying soldier didn't resemble each other, but something in Michail's eyes spoke of tragedy. The young man whose hand she'd held as the stream of life abandoned his vein—he never got to see her hair colour, concealed under the white headdress like a nun's.

His hand opened like a lotus flower (Leticia meanwhile saved a life by sticking her fingers in someone's artery). Childhood seemed so distant but Orla remembered everything, every lotus; Michail's gaze like the lake's green water, and she knew the extent of her intuition—her silent animal wisdom too wordless to lie.

The day they learned about the ship, she'd felt it before anyone else; she couldn't swallow her food and her palms were sweating. It was Leticia to whom Michail gave the note, but only because of her place at the table, closer to where he stood. A mere coincidence, even if it did appear to give Leticia credit for their imminent rescue, as well as the delusion, if her claims that she kissed him in the cellar were true, that she was more experienced in matters of love. "Practise," she'd said, for when they met the cousins in England.

The distant purr of an engine burst from the depths of the forest. Orla's eyes widened on the glass—all windows had, for days now, been covered with newspapers. Her heart pounding that she feared she may have a heart attack. (She didn't want to die. Not yet. Not until she had lived.)

"It's time, Orla!"

Orla heard it loud and clear, even if Leticia only

whispered her reprimand. She helped her undress, like she had a disability, like Orla needed to be dealt with first.

"Mother, do my buttons," she said.

Mother stood behind her and worked on undoing the stiff buttons of her high-neck blouse, listening to her like she was the daughter and Leticia the mother. Orla closed her eyes to the humming of her voice, as if the darkness could drown the fear surging with the nearing car engine. Leticia recited her words like scriptures; there was never any room for doubt and only conviction where she was concerned. This propelled her forward, always forward.

"Father is coming. He's coming with the convoy. We'll be in England soon. England! And we *will* return someday. Not here, but to the palace. It's like mother said, extraordinary things are happening. That is what this is: plans unfolding. We must *never* forget who we are…"

Words. They too were ties keeping Leticia together, just as Orla felt reassured by the pull of silk ribbons, the tight, decisive motions as her sister fastened the corset like armour around her waist. An unbreakable bond. A past Orla would always carry underneath her coveted disguise of mediocrity.

(Sometimes masks are truer than truth.)

"Orla, put your blouse back on."

A loud knocking hit the other side of the door.

Neither Leticia nor the Empress had time to don their own undergarments, but they did manage to throw some of the lose jewels in their pockets and to push the case under the settee before their delay to answer would expose them. The lack of a distinct pause between each one had warned them the knocks hadn't come from Michail's fist, but the strange new soldier's modesty reassured them. Not once did he lift his head as he summoned them downstairs for their transportation, nor did he make an attempt to search them.

They followed him down the staircase and another. Orla caught sight of the outside through a small windowpane, where the newspaper had lifted. An open palm like a flower, too similar to death (and love), lay on the gravel. It lingered in her mind as she went—the hand owner's face was turned away from her, so she didn't see his features—but his unmistakable brown curls, Michail's unmistakeable curls, facing her. The cellar door opening. Reality impaling her with ice-cold fear.

Michail is dead!

The soldier bowed briskly and exited the room. Bare brick walls surrounded them ominously. "He's one of us," said the Empress—her heaving chest contrasting the semblance of confidence.

"Yes," said Leticia. "We're about to escape through

that secret tunnel."

A small door in the wall. Their future on the other side of that door. Leticia saw it with her glass eyes. Her will bouncing right back at her. The light of a definite conviction. A conviction Orla could only envy, but especially the protection which that conviction bestowed upon her. Nothing could hurt her through her glow of self-assurance and optimism.

"Leticia, are you certain?"

"Yes, Mother. There isn't a chair to sit on."

Their voices muted as truth sat sickly at the back of Orla's tongue. She choked, needing to tell them about Michail, but instead retched and bent over in a corner to empty her stomach. Vomit splashed on her shoes, the imprint of his flower-hand flashing green and purple around her as her mother's palm landed on her back for comfort. But only until the doorknob turned—the doorknob on the big door.

The Emperor's face is proud as he enters. Hearts flutter below the modest smiles quivering, but there's a new tension behind him. Armed men bearing an alien tightness of brow and muscle, of jaws protruding and pulsing on their angular faces, as Empress and Princess spurt into his stiff embrace. The circle like a lifesaver drifting. She wipes her mouth with her sleeve.

Threads of Leticia's hair gleam like sunshine against father's coarse lapel despite there being no sun, no manner of slit or crack or opening to let in the slightest form of natural light but that which she alone irradiates, the light beyond which she never sees. How Orla coveted her glass eyes of blindness, as the new soldier returns, but doesn't bow this time. His eyes meet hers. He sees her for a brutal moment, but she's soon nothing but a sheet of newspaper through which he stares at the wall behind her. The dying man in the hospital—he sees through her too, sees the woman he loves in her face and not hers. But that is the fantasy she clings to as the soldier breathes in, readying to utter the dreaded sentence, a piece of paper like parchment in his hand, eternally unrolling.

They all run to Orla as the guns lift. Mouths wide open as their guttural bellows erupt, but all she hears is royal bone breaking, precious stone chipping, lightbulb glass bursting—bodies collapsing around her as hers convulses eternally against the wall.

She is a fish on hot stone, protected by the precious shield of her jewels. Carcasses around her shudder like porcelain; terrible earthquake as the young soldier aims his barrel at her along with the others and the repeated blast of steel pounds against her chest.

She doesn't see the darkness, but she's in it. Running

like a rat in circles around the room, hands covering her ears, waiting for a final deafening explosion that doesn't come. There is no end, only endless circles, fragments fanning and turning.

But suddenly, she faces it. How long has she been running? She stops in the hugest space of her solitude but sees the walls around her, irreparably solid.

Her ethereal skull bleeds on the floor. Broken shells of her family also materialise into their spectral substance. They're not there anymore; they're only memories. Shards of a past like broken glass in the sunshine, to cut her soles at every step. Flashes of darkness hit her too from the sidelines, their corpses dragged by the ankles, blood like scratch marks on the concrete.

The hem of Leticia's skirt floats in the puddle of their blood. Glass eye weeping; a tear like a melted snowflake. Their chests studded with bullets, like gems, protecting them from this horror.

She backs to the wall and lets her knees surrender, slides down against the roughness of brick. She sees gold steam surge beautifully from Leticia's doll corpse, glide to the door in the wall and its bright perimeter of light. Mother, Father, they follow her. Michail is there too, in the steam. They all urge Orla to join them, but the painful sobbing is louder, and she cannot not listen to it.

The tunnel stretches. The soldier curls like an ageing man. His gun hanging from his arm falls thunderously and forever. He bears the echoes like Orla bears the echoes, drops to his knees, buries his face in his shaking hands. Purple vein bulges, hands too much like love.

Sunlight absorbs into the brick as they cross, and she stays. She watches him endlessly—watches it all unfold, time and time again. He looks at their shells, their porcelain faces beautiful in her memory. Not her own—Orla doesn't have a face anymore. He covers the jumble of flesh that is her face with a handkerchief, whispers an internal prayer. He turns to Leticia, his eyes well like the lake on her patent shoes. He plummets on Leticia's body, sobbing, gagging. His weight on her.

How she envies her for that weight. How she covets the weight of earth on her bones, but her palm stretched on the brick, she cannot cross. She can only run in circles to escape the wheel of memories. Waiting for her eyes to glass.

An Infinity of Penance

by Andrea Eaker

After I killed my mother, I stopped drinking. For days, I was nauseated and trembling as I detoxed, smothering in my guilt. Then the trembling faded, and when the nausea had shrunk to just a curl, I realised how I could atone. I would find a universe where Mom was alive, and I was the one who was dead. I would take the place of my dead metaverse self. I would have another chance. This time, I wouldn't take Mom for granted. She'd die happy and old at home, surrounded by my brother's kids, maybe even their children. That's the end she deserved.

I knew exactly when to Jump: an evening a year ago when I left the tavern drunk and crashed my terrapod into a tree. The medics told me I'd nearly died. Of the infinite universes our decisions spawn, it should be easy to find one where my accident was just a bit worse.

When I was finally sober, I found a black-market Jumper. Even after selling everything, I could only afford an early ChronosHead, a model so small I touched both walls when I stretched my arms. I could set the time and place of the accident easily enough, but the universe selection was a crapshoot; the universe dial in these early models was like rolling a marble on an oiled mirror. I set myself one rule: I would only ever turn the dial counterclockwise. That way I would know I wasn't retracing my steps.

After the crash, my brother visited me in the hospital. I was still slurring when I told him I was all right. "Fine," I kept saying. "I'm *fine*."

"I know," he said, biting the syllables so his teeth clicked. "More's the pity."

I didn't learn my lesson. A year later, Mom called to ask if I'd fixed the pressure valve on her finicky heating unit the way she'd asked. I must have agreed, either to get her off my back or because I thought I'd actually done it. The next morning when she turned it on, it flashed back and ignited. It exploded. It burned everything. All of her things, the whole house, the walls that had sheltered us as children. Her, too.

Before the first Jump, I dyed my hair dark and cut it myself, in a raggedy asymmetry that I told myself was edgy. I gave away all my clothes except a few baggy dresses and boots no one was likely to recognise.

The last thing I did in my universe was unscrew the casing of the return button, push free the glass and wire mechanism, and drop it outside the Jumper. I'm not coming back. Why keep something that would bring me back to a place where no one wanted me?

Every Jump, it's twilight. I'm in the woods outside the tavern. The metaverse version of me shows up most of the time, but not always. Whenever I see her approaching, I feel sick with envy for her limitless life, her still-alive mother. I see her and I go thirsty in a way I've never been, not even for alcohol. I want to grind her down and drink her so there's no trace.

But my other self refuses to die. The doctors told me it was a matter of centimetres; if the steering handle had gone just a bit more to the side, I would have bled out within minutes. But whenever she climbs into the terrapod and steers too fast away from the tavern, her accident ends like mine: she staggers from the crushed vehicle with blood swelling from her wounds. Watching her from the woods, I see her bleed and my own scars ache.

I am going to grow old living through this night again and again, hoping the other version of myself will die.

When I'm hungry, I eat at the bar and they don't

recognise me as the same woman drinking a few seats down. My showers come splashed out of the bathroom sink. I sleep in the Jumper's pilot chair. Sometimes I wake up touching the place where the return button used to be.

I don't think about my brother or my mother. I'll think of them when I find the right universe. I won't apologise because Mom won't know what I have to be sorry for. But I will make it up to her every day.

Finally, I look Mom up just to see her image in the query results: her easy big smile, the tiny gap between her front teeth, the lines around her eyes. She's still alive here.

This is taking too long.

I go into the bar and order shots for my metaverse self. I drink with her, one sip for her every three gulps and my body unfurls with the alcohol. I will be sober again. Later.

She is funnier than I am, a bit crasser. She seems even more unhappy than me, even more unhappy than I remember being at my worst.

A few times, she squints as if she might recognise me.

I can do this.

I buy her so much to drink; I have to haul her outside

and push the ignition stick into her hand. "Thanks," she says.

"It's fine," I say, struggling with her terrapod door.

"You listened to me," she mumbles as I drop her into the seat. "No one else does. I'm too lost cause. Too much…too lost cause."

I am leaning into her pod, breathing her scent. It's my own scent, clouded with alcohol. But she smells of something else. An absence of sorrow. Hope. It's faint, but it's there. Another thing to envy, something that she has that I don't.

I take away the ignition stick.

In the tavern, I send an aural request, and when Mom answers, I nearly choke. Her voice sounds just the same. It hits a deep, deep nerve I thought was dead.

I say the name of the tavern where she can come pick up her daughter.

"I will." I could always tell when she was crying. "I'm just glad to know where she is."

"The ignition stick is with the bartender."

She thanks me. Then she says, "You sound just like her."

I could stay. I could wait for her to arrive so I can say it in person. But I know I can't. To see her would release my desperate envy, and I would lose the strength to do the right thing. "I'm sorry," I say, and I disconnect.

Back in the ChronosHead pilot seat, I touch the space where the return button was.

Then I turn the dial to the left, and Jump.

Toxic

by S.O. Green

Mel was too busy ducking bullets and scrambling for the park across the street to look both ways, so it probably wasn't a surprise when she got hit by a car.

The cab picked her up on its hood, carried her ten feet, and dumped her onto the asphalt with a squeal of brakes, like a hypertensive housewife realising there was a spider in her hair. She rolled twice and then waited for the world to stop spinning before she stood up.

She looked at the cab driver, gaping at her through the windshield.

"And that's why road safety is important."

She snatched up the briefcase and limped the rest of the way, thanking God for the invention of leather jackets and denim. Road rash wasn't anyone's friend. She'd reached the gate to the park before she realised she'd dropped her gun.

"Great. Absolutely fucking wonderful. I'm on a roll."

The roll had started when she'd tried to bust two lowlifes trading shady-looking briefcases in a back alley.

Which would have been easier if she'd been an actual cop, and if she'd read the situation right since both guys had been planning to rip each other off and had brought a half-dozen accomplices with them.

At some point during the absolute cluster-fuck that followed, Mel had decided that getting the briefcase full of drugs off the street was a happy second place to her original plan. Only problem was *both* gangs kind of wanted the drugs.

They were still on her tail. Goons in ski masks and stretched ladies' legwear, clutching big guns in meaty hands and looking all around for *her*. But she was almost through the gate, into the park, ready to disappear among the trees and—

"Over there! She's heading into the park!"

Mel sighed. "Crap."

She stumbled towards the fountain, where all the paths converged, hoping she could find a place to hide before they caught up. Part of her was screaming, *drop the fucking case!* But that was loser talk.

By the time she reached the fountain, she was starting to consider a compromise. She could drop the case in the water. Take the drugs out of circulation and maybe take a little focus off herself. It would be satisfying, watching that junk bleeding out into the pool, knowing the gang bangers couldn't do a thing about it.

Unfortunately, she'd forgotten there was more than one entrance into the park. And that her top speed was currently "hobble."

"End of the line, bitch!" one of the thugs by the fountain snapped.

"Hey, I could be really nice for all you know."

Nicer than a drug dealer. Yeah, that was probably a safe bet.

"Give me the fucking case."

"You didn't say please."

He cocked his gun. He still didn't say please.

"Scout's honour you won't shoot me?"

God, if he'd really been a scout then that was a shame. How the mighty had fallen.

He was about two seconds from earning a merit badge for having no sense of humour when the ground erupted under him and tossed him ten feet in the air. He let out a strangled scream, turned a full somersault, and landed on his head on the other side of the fountain.

"Oh shit!" one of his accomplices yelped. "It's Quake!"

Mel sighed. "Great."

Quake didn't dress like a comic book superhero, but she had the pattern right. Case in point: "Come quietly and I won't have to hurt you."

When faced with someone who could manipulate stone with their mind, one of the three remaining crooks made the wise decision to drop his gun and flee. The other two opened fire and gaped when their bullets ricocheted off a wall that hadn't been there two seconds before.

Quake waved a hand and knocked one guy out with a chunk of makeshift wall to the face. The other screamed and crumpled as the ground opened up and bit him in the ankles like an attack dog. It pinned him in place until Quake could close the distance and rattle his jaw with a haymaker that dropped him like…

Well, like a stone.

She didn't need powers for that part. Quake had a punch like a sledgehammer.

By that point, Mel was curled up on the floor, clutching the briefcase to her chest, just *waiting* for what was coming.

"What the hell are you doing out here, Mel?"

She muttered an answer, like a child on the naughty step.

"Huh?"

"I said, 'I was trying to help'! Okay? How the hell did you even know?"

Quake shrugged. "Bad vibes. Seriously, Mel, were

you *trying* to get yourself killed?"

"Oh please. I was doing fine, it was just…more complicated than I thought."

"That's why I use my *superpowers* when I fight crime, Mel. Do you have any superpowers?"

Mel shook her head. Other than an uncanny ability to overestimate her own abilities and a best friend with elemental control of stone, no, she didn't.

"Go home, Mel. Please. I don't want you to get hurt. Just leave this to me. I don't need…"

Mel's head snapped up. "Don't need what? Don't need me?"

"That's not what I was going to say. I worry about you, Mel. You keep getting yourself into trouble, and what happens if I'm not there to save you?"

"I can take care of myself."

"Damn it, Mel!"

Was it her imagination, or did the earth move?

"Taking care of yourself doesn't mean knowing how to throw a punch or shoot a gun. It means keeping yourself *out* of dangerous situations in the first place."

"Yeah, no problem, Mom."

Quake took a breath. The floor trembled with sympathetic awkwardness. She was, literally, quaking with anger.

Everyone who'd stopped to gawk probably thought they *were* mother and daughter. Except they were the same age and, until a few months ago, Mel had been the impressive one. Athletic, smart, creative, business-savvy.

But she didn't have any superpowers.

She was starting to wonder if maybe this was how Tess had felt. Overshadowed. Outshined.

Jealous.

"Give me the briefcase, Mel."

She fought an overwhelming urge to toss it in the fountain. A last-ditch effort to maintain some self-respect.

She handed her the briefcase and said nothing.

"Go home."

Quake marched off. More crime to fight. More people to save. She couldn't babysit Mel all night. More important things to do.

Mel scrubbed her eyes, pushed herself up, and wondered if there was a chance in hell her gun might still be there. Instead, she walked the other way. Towards home. Like she'd been told.

"Damn, that was pretty awkward."

There was a girl sitting on the wall. Long, black hair and porcelain pale skin. Halter top and denim cut-offs, a belt thicker than her arms, and boots that could have stomped out socialist revolutions in South American countries. She swept her fringe out of her eyes and favoured Mel with a sympathetic smile.

"Eavesdropping much?"

"It's not eavesdropping if you're shouting."

"It wasn't a public show, and I *don't* need a review from the peanut gallery."

"I'm not trying to pick a fight with you, I just…feel bad for you."

"Huh?"

"I saw what you were trying to do. You wanted to help. What she said wasn't fair. It's not your fault you don't have powers."

Mel pursed her lips. She didn't know what she hated more. Feeling her friendship with Tess slipping away, or a complete stranger understanding her better than her best friend.

"No offence, but I don't even know you."

"The name's Trip."

Mel groaned. "You're one of them, aren't you?"

"The name gave it away, huh?"

"Yeah, pretty much. So what's your power?"

"Illusions," she announced and swirled her hands. Neon butterflies danced out of her palms. "Pretty useless, right?"

"More useless than no powers at all?"

"It's not exactly encasing people in solid rock or creating shields out of the ground, is it?"

"Amen, sister."

Trip hopped down off the wall. "You want to go grab a coffee, maybe?"

***

"So, you guys were friends for two years *before* all this 'Quake' stuff started?"

Mel stared into the Americano she'd ordered. Probably a bad choice, considering how late it was, but she needed something to push back the stiffness in her body after her tango with the concrete. She'd checked herself out in the bathroom mirror. Bruised real good, but nothing broken.

She'd hurt her pride more than anything.

Trip had paid for the coffee. She'd been insistent, because the white chocolate mocha monstrosity she'd ordered cost about triple what a black coffee did.

So, there she was having coffee with a superhero. She'd never had coffee with Quake.

"Yeah. Shared an apartment and everything. We spent a lot of time together. I worked from home, she only played in the evening, so…"

"Netflix and pizza?"

"Pretty much. We had a lot of good times."

Of course, that depended on who you asked, right? Mel, with the string of successful tech start-ups, the business degree, and the bestselling book on management philosophy? Or Tess, whose band only earned enough every night to pay for beer and who'd just managed to escape the relationship from hell?

Literally from hell, judging by the burn scars on her back.

Those times had been good for Mel, because everything was a matter of perspective and you felt so high when the person beside you was so low. And it made her sick; how badly she wished she was back up there again.

"But it's over now?"

"Sure feels like it. We don't hang out anymore. I mean, I know she's working really hard, the cops are struggling, the city's going to shit, but…"

"Feels like she's doing too much? Like she won't make time for the things she used to enjoy?"

"I guess it makes me wonder if she *ever* enjoyed it."

Maybe she hadn't. Could she blame her for that? Sitting on the couch with the movie paused while Mel took a conference call? Dinner plans cancelled because

Mel suddenly had a date? Spending her whole life on hold, waiting for someone else.

This was probably what she deserved.

"And you just want to help."

"I want to be a part of her new life. I want us to be friends like we used to be. If she can't go back to the way things were, maybe *I* can go forward."

"Only she won't let you."

"She keeps telling me to stay home. *How* am I supposed to stay home?"

"Don't take it personally. You know Tess. She doesn't even want the cops trying to fight criminals in case they get hurt and that's their *job*."

They shared a laugh. A warm little chuckle at the caricature that was their friend.

Except…

"She never mentioned you."

"Probably not. She never mentioned you either."

Sting. Mel busied herself with coffee, trying not to take it personally.

"Can I level with you? About the powers thing?" Trip set her coffee down, took a deep breath. "It's bullshit. We didn't get our powers because we earned them or because we deserved them. We got out powers because some *thing* out there, beyond all this, poked a hole through reality and ran its slimy, little fingers across our minds. That's all. It's not a gift. It's…compensation."

"Tess told me people got powers based on what they were good at."

"Not exactly. It's called the Affinity Phenomenon. Our powers are based on things we understand. Quake's powers are vibrations because she was a drummer."

"Makes sense, I guess."

It didn't. It didn't make any sense, because something had reached through the fabric of existence and doled out powers to people for no goddamn reason. It had pointed at randoms, and said, "you're special." It had pointed at Tess and not Mel.

And, God help her, she couldn't stand it.

Trip had picked up a coffee stirrer and was using it to write her name in neon in the air. It burned in Mel's eyes like a sparkler wand.

She'd have given anything to have powers of her own right at that moment.

"You ever heard of an Inversion Capsule?" Trip asked.

"Hell no."

"I don't know much about them, really. The science is pretty complex. Malleus created them."

"The villain, Malleus?"

"Not anymore. He died a while back. Took all the powers he'd stolen with him. Dark days. Quake was there."

"Really?"

She'd kept that quiet.

"Apparently…"

Trip lowered her voice, leaned in. Suddenly, Mel was in a gangster movie. Wasn't the all-night diner the venue of choice for life-changing revelations and schemes?

"Apparently, you can use them to transfer powers between people."

"Lucky them."

"I mean, people without powers. You know Malleus was powerless, right? Until he created the capsule."

"I didn't know."

She could understand, though. Building a device like that, just to taste it.

"Too bad I'm not a genius. I could whip one up. Trade places with Quake for a month or two."

Trip smiled. "Or you could just use mine."

***

Trip gave her the capsule and told her how to use it—*monstrously* simple—but then came the hard part. Getting

Quake somewhere safe to make the transfer.

"We should hang out," Mel told her over the phone. "Grab some pizza, watch a movie. Talk about things. Like old times."

"Mel, people need me."

"It's just one night."

"A lot can happen in one night."

"Yeah, but…I miss you."

That did it. And it made Mel feel like a tool but, as Trip said, "We're helping her. She'll burn out eventually. Superheroes need holidays."

So she ordered the pizza and picked the movie and waited and wondered, not for the first time, if this was how it had felt to be Tess just six months ago. Sitting home, waiting for your best friend to cancel.

She didn't cancel. Quake took off her jacket at the door and kicked off her boots. She padded through in threadbare socks and a Gameboy tee, like the Tess of old.

"I brought beer," she said, holding up a six-pack.

"Great."

Maybe she could have waited, enjoyed the night, since she was taking their friendship and smashing it against the wall. She knew it, no matter how she tried to spin it. But she couldn't sit there and smile, knowing what was going to happen.

Mel twisted the capsule, and the room filled with high-pitched whining.

Six beer bottles fell and smashed on the floor. Tess staggered, trying to keep her feet, then toppled over, taking the TV with her. She hit the floor and clutched her stomach like she'd been stabbed. Should have been her back.

Mel gaped at her, horror growing. Something was pouring into her. Something warm in her chest, stretching out into her limbs like a hand into a glove.

Was this how it felt to be powerful? Did it always make you feel so sick?

"Holy shit!"

"Mel, what the fu—?!"

"It wasn't supposed to hurt. I don't—"

"Of course it hurts."

This from Trip, who'd appeared in the doorway like she'd been there all along. She smiled at Mel. Actually, it was a sneer.

"You're ripping out a piece of who she is. Her affinity. Think of it like tearing out her heart while it's still beating. Some of us already know how that feels. Right, Tess?"

Tess looked up at her. There was so much pain in her eyes, but there was still room for recognition. She said one word. One name.

"Lacey?"

Mel gaped. "*She's* your ex?"

"I'm not her ex," Trip snarled. "Because she's still mine."

She seized Mel around the throat. They were about the same build, so there was no lifting her into the air with one hand. But there was squeezing, crushing pressure around her windpipe and, suddenly, she was on her knees.

Mel wrapped both hands around Trip's wrist, tried to pry her off. She wasn't strong enough. She called Quake's power, but she couldn't feel it. Not even a tremor.

It wasn't her affinity. She didn't understand it, didn't *know* it the way Tess did. She'd stolen it and she couldn't even *use* it.

"You see why illusions are useless? All you have to do is tell the right person the right thing and they'll believe whatever you say. I don't need a light show for that."

"If you wanted her power…"

"I don't give a shit about her power. I've been watching you for two years. *Two years!* You think I didn't see what was going on? All those little smiles? The looks you gave each other? Brushing past each other in the kitchen or the hallway? You think you can take what's mine?"

"We weren't…we never…I'm not…"

"*Bullshit!* You're fucking *lying!*"

"Lacey," Tess breathed. There were tears in her eyes and she was quivering with pain. But she wasn't afraid for herself. As usual. "Please. Don't."

"You don't get to ask me for anything, Tess. Why did you leave? We could have talked it out."

"No. We couldn't. You'd have twisted me up. You *always* twisted *everything*."

Trip's eyes were hollow. Her grip was tightening. "You always made me out to be the bad guy. But I'm not the one who betrayed you."

Mel could see lights behind her eyes. She didn't think it was one of Trip's illusions. She was going to die.

She looked at Tess, lying in the wreckage of their living room and their friendship. She breathed the only last words that mattered.

I'm sorry…

Like a Mermaid

by Neen Cohen

Lena pushed her head up through the surface of the water. She flung her long dark ponytail back and smiled over at the lane beside her. Her heart raced beneath her swimmers, knowing this time she had beaten the girl in the next lane.

Twelve years before, she'd chosen this specific public pool for its name and the recognition it gave its fastest swimmers.

For years, her smiling face had been at the top of the leader board, and it would be back there again.

Her smile slipped.

The show-off was already sitting on the edge of the pool, taking off her swimming cap. Her blonde hair tumbled out of the black plastic, long fingers pulling it over her shoulder to squeeze out the few drops that had made it through the barrier.

"You're getting so much faster, Lena. Well done."

"Thanks, Hannah," she muttered and held on to the bar beneath the starting block. Water caressed Hannah's defined arms and muscled legs as she stood up in one swift movement. She balanced unwaveringly on the edge of the pool; she might as well be walking on the water. Hannah kissed her girlfriend, who wrapped the towel around her shoulders.

"Come on, top mermaid. Let's go get some breakfast."

Lena watched them head to the showers and scoffed.

"Real mermaids don't wear bathing caps."

She waited a moment to ensure she was out of sight before swimming to the ladder to get out.

As more of her body was pulled out of the water, her weight pulled down on her limbs.

They wore the same swimmers.

Lena had gone and bought her own pair when Hannah had shown up in her new silver and black size 8 version.

There was no one there to wrap Lena's towel around her shoulders or body, or a size 16 neon green swimmers. It was the only colour in her size.

It wasn't fair.

Lena trained more hours and ate healthier, but still Hannah had just showed up six months ago and had beaten her every morning before she flitted off to her perfect life.

Every day, Lena imagined different ways Hannah's perfect day could go horribly wrong.

She didn't want Hannah to die, where was the pleasure in knowing her pain was ended. She just wanted her to suffer tremendously, and for her to see Lena skip forward in this world, back in the top spot where she belonged.

"They keep getting younger and faster, don't they, Lena?" John was a stupid man who insisted on flirting with Lena every chance he got. His button-down uniform shirt strained against his swollen, hairy belly as he tucked it unsuccessfully back into his pants where the band disappeared beneath the overhang of self-indulgent flesh. The logo over the top pocket of his shirt had changed over the years. But Lena could always find the mermaid, even in the more modern-day stylised pattern.

"She's not any faster, John." Lena spat his name as she pulled the towel tighter over her generous breasts. "I allow the young ones to feel good about themselves. Heaven knows how they would feel about a forty-year-old beating them, even if I do still pass for being in my thirties."

John raised his eyebrows with a smirk on his lips.

Lena took it for more flirting. The man never gave her a break.

"Well, all I know is that she's just been signed to the national team. It's a big accomplishment."

"Oh"—Lena forced a smile—"how nice for her."

Lena didn't bother going into the showers: she didn't

want to see that smug face again today.

It was a 25-minute drive from the pools to Lena's home. She passed several other pools on her drive, but not one of them compared to Mermaids.

By the time Lena pulled into her garage, her car stank of the chlorine from the pool water.

Just another thing Hannah had done to destroy her life.

Lena deserved to be a household name, not that degenerate and her patronising arrogance. All these years and after six months, that waif was going to be on the national swim team.

Lena closed the door between the garage and her laundry harder than necessary.

She carefully peeled off her swimmers and put them directly into the washing machine before walking to the bathroom and into the shower. Oh, how she would have been scolded for doing this once upon a time.

Stepping out of the water, Lena found herself angrier rather than less.

How dare that little twig of a girl come into her town, into her pool, and parade around as though she were a real mermaid?

Real mermaids didn't exist.

Lena looked around her living room at the ceramic mermaids that covered most surfaces. When Jolie, the woman she never called mother, died, Lena had begun her collection. But the real prize of her house was the lap pool that shared a clear wall with her living room. It was money well spent, left from a woman who had never had to work a day in her life. Lena smiled every time she looked at it, knowing Jolie's body continued to rot and wither beneath the concrete slab of Lena's pool.

When Lena was seven, Jolie told her daughter that she could have a special treat for passing her first witch's test. Lena could still remember the pounding of her heart inside her chest as she has whispered into Jolie's ear.

"A mermaid. I want my very own mermaid."

"You stupid child." Jolie had laughed and smacked the young one across the head. "How did you pass your first test if you still think mermaids are real? Mermaids aren't real. You are an idiot."

Lena clenched her teeth until her jaw hurt as she thought about this and many other abusive memories of her past.

But who was laughing now?

Lena had her water and her mermaids.

She would be the strongest swimmer at the pools again soon enough. She just had to figure out how.

Brushing her fingers gently over several of the mermaids' hairs, Lena moved passed them and into her bedroom. The multitude of ceramic mermaids in here cluttered every surface, taking up every available spot. These were her precious ones. Visitors, not that she had any, wouldn't be able to knock any of these beauties with their clumsiness.

There was a ceramic mermaid, a new one that had long golden curls and sat in the middle of her dressing table.

She hadn't decided where the young, slim sprite should go yet. It was familiar, and Lena felt the anger build inside her chest again.

Before she knew it, she stood in front of her broken mirror—her new acquisition decapitated amongst the shattered glass.

A smile spread across Lena's face as she picked up the broken head.

"Looks like you need a new tail, little mermaid."

Lena felt much calmer as she picked up her sewing box and headed out to the living room to watch tv as she did some sewing.

She placed the broken head on her coffee table as she began a new sewing project. That woman, the one she never called mother, had taught her how to sew. Had insisted upon it.

Lena was grateful for the specialised knowledge she

now used.

***

For the first time in years, Lena wasn't at the pools.

For the rest of the week, she did little else but work on her sewing project.

Her fingers sparked with each thread her needles took, colours weaving from her mouth as she pressed the enchanted words into each stitch.

By Sunday night, she hummed happily as she finished the task at hand and got her bag ready for the pool in the morning.

The Monday morning drive was perfect, the full moon beginning to fade, and Lena knew it was a sign. The energies were aligning, and things would all work out her way.

Perfectly predictable, Hannah was out the front of the pool doors when Lena walked up. The sun wasn't quite up yet, and no other swimmers would arrive until well into Lena and Hannah's lap.

Lena's swimming bag was slightly heavier than normal on her forearm, but nothing was going to stop her from smiling.

"Lena, it's so good to see you. We were starting to

worry that you might be sick."

"Oh no, dear." Lena patted Hannah on the forearm. "Just very busy."

"Oh, that's a relief," Hannah said.

"Is your friend here yet?"

"No, she likes her sleep-ins. But she will be happy to see you when she comes to pick me up."

"Lovely."

Lena smiled and pushed her shoulders back further; a small smile played at the corner of her lips as the pool doors were opened by the early staff, allowing them inside. The staff barely grunted to her and Hannah as they turned back to get class equipment set up, barely registering who they let in.

Perfect.

Lena's heart pounded in her chest. She struggled to keep her steps even as her fingers trembled. It took three times before successfully turning the handle of her own shower.

Closing her eyes, the running water helped soothe the edge of her nerves. She waited until she heard the second shower run. A few more moments later, the metal rings scraping against the cubicle railing told Lena it was time to move.

Fully clothed, Lena opened her bag and gingerly

pulled out the filled syringe. She shouldn't need all of it, but it was better to have extra on hand. It was a long trip home.

Hannah was humming as she washed herself down, readying herself for the morning's laps. Laps she would never do.

Lena caught her reflection in the length of mirror above the sinks and watched as her smile broke her face in half.

It was time to begin. She had thought about and memorised every step and every word.

Every reaction she had perfected to their predictable questions and worries.

She could of course had done it the easy way, Jolie's way. Using her magical skills for the entire thing.

But where was the fun in that?

There was something far more satisfying by playing by their rules and still beating them.

Lena pulled back the curtain.

Hannah turned, her head cocked and her eyebrows knitting as she looked at Lena.

Lena frowned, disappointed at Hannah's lack of fear, but there was time for that yet.

"Did you forget something, Lena? Do you need to borrow something?"

How could this harlot be so unashamed of her naked body, seen by a virtual stranger?

"No, dear, just wanted to make sure you were clean before I took you."

"What?"

Not quite fear, but the confusion on Hannah's face put a little more enthusiasm in Lena's movements.

The syringe slid so easily into Hannah's naked flesh. Lena took pleasure in plunging the syringe into Hannah's perfect breast. She hesitated before giving the plunger a little extra push. That would buy Lena a few more hours.

Lena let the thin body collapse to the ground, chuckling when a sickening crack echoed around the tiles.

She walked with a small skip in her step and turned off her own shower. Only one shower running will be enough.

There was no point in wasting more water.

Lena knew the entire complex more intimately than the young ones, even more than the current workers.

No one had wondered why her car was parked out the back today.

Self-centred creatures.

Knowing she had plenty of time, Lena calmly spread out Hannah's bag, a few objects she gently rolled across the floor.

After surveying her crime scene, Lena wrapped Hannah's unconscious body in the ridiculously small towel she used. Lena cradled Hannah in her arms, heading for her car as though the small child had merely fallen asleep while out and it was time to go home.

She had been underestimated for so many years now.

But that didn't matter any longer.

She was finally going to complete her collection.

Unceremoniously dumping Hannah in her boot, she returned to the showers.

There was no need to rush. She could use a nice swim.

Her time lit up on the big electronic boards at the end of her laps, and she pulled herself out of the pool without needing the ladder. She hadn't felt this strong in years.

As she drove out, she waved to Hannah's girlfriend who was looking around, panic beginning to swell in her eyes.

***

Lena hummed as she sat at the edge of her lap pool.

The sun was almost setting; colours splashed across the surface of the pool, rippling with the gentle breeze.

"What's going on?" Hannah tried lifting her head and let out an almighty scream of pain. It echoed around Lena's backyard, bouncing off the eight-foot-high brick fences and splashing against the water. The neighbours wouldn't hear a thing, they never did. Jolie had made sure of that when she first cast the dampening field over the house. Lena was grateful it had survived Jolie's death.

"What's happening?" Hannah's voice came out in a choked sob.

"I'm making all your dreams come true."

Lena smiled at Hannah as though she were offering the younger woman a piece of apple pie from her windowsill.

She looked old enough to be Hannah's grandmother, now more than ever.

"What have you done?" Tears slid down Hannah's temples as she tried to move again without success.

"I'm making you a mermaid, of course."

Hannah looked up and screamed. Lena was pleased her placement of the large mirror was correct.

Lena shushed her and gently stroked some sticky wisps of hair from Hannah's face.

"It took a long time to make you perfect, Hannah. The least you can do is appreciate the effort."

Hannah sobbed and closed her eyes, shutting out her reflection.

Lena looked at the shuddering body and admired her

handiwork.

Hannah's breasts had been sheared from her body and replaced with clam shells that took Lena longer then she had expected. Sewing through shell wasn't easy, especially when the flesh beneath was bloody and raw. Lena had had to get a bucket of water to rinse her hands after every other stitch, her fingers getting sticky from the leaking blood. But the effort had been worth it. The shells replaced Hannah's perk little titties with such beauty in their off-white colouring.

But the real piece de resistance was the amorphization of Hannah's legs. The tail glistened with rainbows of colours, reflecting the sunset.

Being a witch had never played much of a role in Lena's life. Jolie, mother dearest, had pushed her to learn the craft, but Lena had never needed it before now.

Each stitch she had sewn had been weaved with the knowledge and energy of her past and magic.

Lena smiled and admired her greatest prize, the greatest mermaid of her collection.

Hannah's legs were encased in the pouch she had spent the week sewing.

The magic vibrated through the material as Lena's chanting infused with Hannah's body, one stitch at a time, destroying the human make up beneath.

One stitch.

The needle of magic pierced into Hannah's skin, through flesh and bone, destroying what it touched as it passed through and out the other side, finding the sewing beneath.

Lena laughed as Hannah screamed again before passing out.

Sweat beaded on Lena's forehead as Hannah came in and out of consciousness. The begging became desperation, which turned to threats and then to nonsensical babbles of agony.

The transformation was finally completed.

Lena sat back on her ankles, her back cracking as she stretched her tight muscles.

Hannah was beautiful.

Lena took one last look at her beautiful creation before she pushed Hannah's body into the pool and before dragging the heavy plastic cover over the top and securing it for the winter.

Inside, Lena sat in her living room, a drink in her hand, and waited.

Finally, Hannah's tail flicked once, and then twice.

The Favourite

by Destiny Eve Pifer

Veronica leaned back in her favourite antique chair and listened to the chaos in the next room. She could hear her mother fussing over her older and more beautiful sister, Jeannie. It was sickening how much they doted on Jeannie, but at the same time, it felt like the sharp blade of a knife being shoved deeper into Veronica's heart.

She was the forgotten one. The strange one who didn't fit in to the perfect family.

For as long as she could remember, Jeannie was always the favourite. She was always the one everyone turned to and whom everyone seemed to just adore.

However, for Veronica, she was the enemy. The one she was determined to bring down. Though she had overlooked the constant favouritism many times, it was the most recent betrayal that made Jeannie her biggest enemy.

In two days, Jeannie would be marrying the only man that Veronica had ever loved. The man she was supposed to be with, but who immediately fell under Jeannie's spell. No one cared about Veronica's heartbreak or how much hurt she felt every time she saw them together. No, they only cared about Jeannie's happiness.

Since the moment she had heard of their wedding plans, Veronica silently had plotted the couple's downfall. She silently plotted the downfall of so many who had hurt her. She rose from her chair and went to check on the happy bunch in the next room. Several times her mother had asked her what she planned to contribute to the wedding since she refused to take any part in it. Jeannie of course had made a show of asking her to be a bridesmaid, but Veronica knew it was merely an act. After all, to everyone else, Jeannie was a sweet and perfect young woman, but to Veronica, she was vindictive and cold.

"I'll bake the wedding cake," Veronica had told her surprised parents. Everyone knew how artistic Veronica was and she was even willing to do it for free.

On the day of the wedding, Veronica stood in the back of the church and listened to the loving vows. As much as she hated Jeannie, she also envied her for having everything Veronica did not.

At the reception, Veronica kept away from everyone and hid in the dark shadows, smoking one cigarette after another. She listened as the happy couple started to cut the cake, she tightened her squeeze on the cigarette until it started to crumble and burn in her hand.

With nothing left but paper and ashes, she walked out to her car and patiently waited. An hour later, her phone began to buzz with desperate texts from her mother. Something was horribly wrong with the cake, and now everyone was ill.

She could see her father stumbling out of the door and towards her car. Just the sight of him practically falling to his knees brought a smile to her face. She stepped out of the car and walked towards him.

He was now vomiting uncontrollably on the pavement. "What have you done?" he asked, trying to raise his head but finding it hard.

"I put a special ingredient in the wedding cake. Did you enjoy it, Daddy?"

Before he could answer, she stepped over him and walked inside. Bodies lay across the reception hall in their own vomit. She walked over to the wedding table and found what remained of her loving sister and brother-in-law. Both had choked on their own vomit and blood.

It was the most glorious sight.

A Normal Little Boy

by Wondra Vanian

The sound of children's squeals clashed with the sound of clattering balls and futuristic laser zappers to give Chloe a monster migraine that wanted to eat her brain. She didn't think she would ever be able to enter a Chuck E. Cheese's again, once this ordeal was over.

Chloe didn't look around for her husband; it was his job to remain anonymous. Instead, she kept her eyes peeled for the perfect opportunity. A couple gathered up their children and prepared to leave the restaurant/indoor play area. They had a boy about the right age but, as they got closer, Chloe realised that he was too fair—all wheat-blonde hair and blue eyes. She turned her attention elsewhere.

Her own child, Noah, dozed in his stroller. Chloe was grateful for the crushed sleeping pill in his bottle of formula that kept him that way; she was certain his incessant wailing, added to the already maddening din, would push her right over the edge.

Had. Noah's incessant wailing *had* pushed her over the edge. Why else would she be there, planning to do

303

what she was planning to do? If Chloe hadn't already been pushed as far as she could possibly go—and further—there was no way her conscious would allow her to commit such an atrocity.

But, like the rest of Chloe, her conscious was tired. So goddamned tired.

She was tired of the crying, tired of the endless stream of doctors' appointments, tired of the support meetings, tired of the well-meaning (but often misguided) advice of family and friends, tired of existing on four hours of sleep a night, tired of the sympathetic looks from strangers—tired, tired, *tired*! Chloe was just too tired to do any of it anymore. So, she gritted her teeth, ordered another cup of coffee, and settled down to endure yet another hour of skull-shattering noise.

Her eye was caught by a dark-haired toddler who pulled on his mother's arm, leading her towards the ball pit. They passed near enough to Chloe for her to see that his eyes were green: a shade or two darker than her husband's but close enough that no one would ask questions. Perfect! Chloe pulled out her cell phone and typed out a quick text.

Found him.

The little boy stood amid the sea of plastic balls, watching the other children as they tossed them in the air with the unchecked glee that comes with not caring what other people think of you. He didn't join their antics, just watched them with his head cocked to the side. The mother sat nearby, but Chloe didn't try to strike up a conversation. She didn't want to be remembered.

Mesmerised by the little boy, Chloe couldn't take her eyes off him as he waded through the balls, following his movements as he climbed up a rope ladder behind an older boy. What would it be like to have a son who could walk on his own? Who could move freely, without every movement causing him pain? Who could play, as children play, without a care?

She couldn't wait to find out.

There was some sort of tussle at the top of the climbing frame, and both boys came tumbling down. The older boy immediately burst into tears, sobbing loudly that he had been pushed. His mother ran over and scooped him up. Chloe risked a glance at the dark-haired boy's mother, who raised a hand to her mouth. Her face wore an expression of horror.

The younger boy didn't look injured, thankfully. He didn't even cry, only watched as the other boy was taken away. *That* boy was obviously hurt; he clutched his arm to his chest and wailed all the way to the door. His mother spoke soothingly to him as she ushered him from the building, siblings in tow.

Chloe didn't worry about staring at the dark-haired boy and his mother—everyone stared. Several uniformed teens were on hand in an instant, offering assistance and robotic apologies, but both mothers waved them off. The mother of the older boy looked hassled, while the other looked…well, terrified.

She thought she understood how the woman felt; it wasn't a long way to fall, but the boy was so very small. At the same time, Chloe was selfishly relieved that the boy was unharmed. Even better, the commotion following the accident could only help draw attention away from Chloe.

It was almost as if God himself had blessed their plan.

The other mother walked towards her son slowly, as if her feet had suddenly turned to bags of sand and she was having trouble lifting them off the floor. Just as slowly, she bent to pick him up. She didn't say a word, just buckled him into a stroller, which was, as if fate had ordained it, similar enough to Chloe's that they might be mistaken.

Her pulse raced. This was it! Chloe fumbled with her phone, adrenaline making it hard to type. One word. Three letters.

Now.

Legs shaking so hard she was surprised she could stand, she quickly pushed Noah's stroller towards the woman and her child. Chloe tugged a toy free, a stuffed cow. Noah loved cows.

"Excuse me?"

Her voice sounded tiny and afraid.

Stupid! she cursed herself. *You've practised this a hundred times. Don't fuck it up now.*

"Excuse me, Ma'am?"

The woman turned around. Chloe's heart pounded so loudly in her chest, she thought everyone would be able to hear it. With a trembling hand, she held out the toy.

"You dropped this."

A look of confusion crossed the other woman's face. "No," she said. "I don't think so…"

Her hands still rested on the handle of the stroller. If she didn't move them, she would ruin everything. Out of the corner of her eye, Chloe could see her husband approaching.

"I'm sure you did," Chloe said in a rush. "It fell out of your bag." She pointed to the bag over the woman's shoulder for good measure.

Chloe held her breath and…the woman released the stroller. She opened the bag and started to root around inside it.

Quicker than she could have thought possible, Chloe's husband was there, swinging one stroller out of the way and leaving the other in its place. The exchange couldn't have taken more than a minute but, for Chloe, it felt like forever. Her eyes darted frantically between the two, certain that the woman would look up at just the wrong moment and catch them in the act. But she didn't.

"No," the other mother insisted, closing the bag and sliding it back over her shoulder. "Definitely not mine."

Relief made Chloe giddy. She laughed, a shrill, nervous sound, and said, "Oh! My mistake! I'll just hand it in to lost and found." Then, she took hold of the stroller in front of her and started walking.

She was tense, waiting for the cry of alarm. The shout that would accuse her of being what she was: a kidnapper. The moment drew out, impossibly long.

There was no shout. No cry.

It was working!

Chloe couldn't believe it. It was too easy. Any moment now, the woman would realise that the stroller she pushed wasn't her own. She would look inside and see an unfamiliar face. They would be made. They would go down. Noah would be put into protective custody. (That, at least, would be a relief.)

But, no, somehow it all went according to plan. Minutes later, Chloe was rounding a corner, rushing over to the van parked beside the building. She was opening the door, hurriedly removing the little boy from the stroller, putting him into the waiting car seat while her husband folded up the stroller and loaded it into the back of the van. Then, she was climbing into the front seat. They were taking off, eyes glued to the rear-view mirror, watching, waiting.

The drive took forever. They'd picked a town over fifty miles away, to reduce the chances of being recognised. Smart, though it meant an agonising trip home down back roads, on a twisting, zigzagging course. The toddler in the back seat didn't make a sound the whole time. Chloe was afraid, at first, that she'd dreamed the whole thing, that when she turned around, Noah would be there, sound asleep, in the car seat. She had to keep turning in her seat to make sure it had really happened.

The little boy with the green eyes and black hair looked back at her, his expression curious rather than frightened.

Finally—*finally!*—they pulled into their driveway. They got out of the car, went around to the side door, opened it, and looked down at their new son. Chloe looked up into her husband's eyes which, like hers, were misty. He smiled at her, and she fell into his arms.

The child looked from one to the other in silence.

***

It didn't take Margaret long to realise that the stroller she was pushing wasn't hers. She stopped, right in the middle of the bustling room, and walked around the stroller. Looking down, she saw a little boy with dark hair.

But not *her* little boy.

The world stopped. At least, hers did. The busy restaurant might as well have not existed for all Margaret knew. She didn't hear the cacophony of children playing, didn't notice the frustrated parents pushing past her, was oblivious to everything except the little boy in the stroller.

What?

How?

Margaret thought, frantically trying to think of what could have happened, of how she could have made such a mistake. Then she remembered the woman—a tired-looking thing with anxious eyes—asking if she'd dropped a toy. Had that woman pushed a stroller too? Margaret wasn't sure. She'd been so preoccupied with the "accident" in the ball pit.

God, another *accident.*

The other woman had probably just stopped too and found herself staring into a stroller at a little boy who was a complete stranger to her. Maybe. Maybe Margaret was wrong, and that she hadn't been pushing a stroller. The place was packed with mothers and their children. The only one Margaret had really noticed was the one undoubtedly on her way to the hospital. She shuddered.

Either she'd been so distracted that she'd mixed up the strollers and the other woman would be back any minute in a panic, or Gabriel was still in the building and Margaret had nearly walked away with someone else's child. She turned and slowly walked back through the building. Back through the indoor play area. Not like she'd lost her child—like she wanted to take one last look at the place.

Margaret didn't call Gabriel's name. She didn't stop any of the frazzled employees to enlist their help. Instead, she casually peeked into strollers, watched children climbing out of plastic tubes, glanced under tables. There was no sign of her son anywhere. This time, when Margaret walked towards the exit, she kept walking.

Margaret walked straight to her car. She opened the door, lifted the sleeping child from his stroller, eased him into the car seat, and buckled him in without waking him. After folding the stroller and putting it into the trunk,

Margaret got into the car. Started the ignition. Drove. Didn't look back until she pulled into her own driveway. Somewhere along the way, the tears started.

Then the laughter—wild, uncontrollable whoops that seemed even wilder because of the tears that streamed down her cheeks.

She knew she was probably in shock, but the relief was more than Margaret could take. Finally. *Finally!* Her prayers had been answered. No more worrying about what her child would light on fire with his eyes. No more living in fear of him revealing what he really was to strangers. No more dread over the day that he really came into his powers.

No more. No more.

A little voice in the back of her head told Margaret that she *should* be worried. What if Gabriel's father returned one day to claim his son? What if this little boy's real parents launched a manhunt for him? All that mattered in that instant, though, was that she had a *normal* little boy, which was all she had ever wanted.

by Zoey Xolton

Lucifer watched Eve draw water from the well, a devious smile creeping to his lips. She was beautiful—but then, all of God's creations were—with green eyes and waist-length hair the colour of honey. She was the light to Lilith's dark. Adam's mate reminded him of Anael, the Archangel of Love, and his first love. Having lost her with his Fall, he sought to fill the void her absence had created.

Lilith was a delicious partner, dark like him, in beauty and in heart. She was his ideal match in many ways—made an exquisite queen of Hell—and yet he pined after Anael and her warm golden light. He wanted what he couldn't have, as was always the case, and deep in his heart, he felt envy. *Why should Adam possess such splendour?* he thought. *What has he done to earn such beauty?*

Adam was no better than he. Adam was mortal, a creature of dirt and dust—unjustly given the gift of freewill—and he had sinned! Alongside his wife, he had been exiled from Eden to brave the world at large and forge a life outside the perfection of the Garden. Instead of supping upon bountiful fruits, swimming in crystal lakes, and lazing on grassy knolls, he was toiling in the filth from which he came. The irony was nothing short of divine.

Existence outside of God's perfect, walled construct was arduous and cruel—the weather fickle, the beasts of the wild dangerous. Yet he felt for Eve, after all, it had been he who had planted the seed of rebellion in her mind. She was gentle and passive—she had not the passion of Lilith whose flames he needed only to stoke.

Why does God forbid you from partaking of the fruit? he had asked Eve, as he'd slithered among the tree's lush branches. *If He loves you so, why does He keep secrets? Why does He exalt Adam above thee?* His questions had festered, eating away at her, devouring her will—day by day—until she felt the fire of curiosity rotting away at her core.

In her search for the truth, she defied God and had partaken of the Fruit of Good and Evil, damning herself, her mate, and her progeny forever more. His plan had worked. Eve had been inaccessible to him in the Garden. Now, he could have her—claim her—and enact the first stage of his master ploy: to birth two races of his own making, both of whom would fight alongside him at the End of Days, and punish God for his failings as a father.

"Eve?"

Eve turned, dropping the pail at the sound of the unfamiliar male voice. Before her stood an angel—for surely he could be nothing else—of such brilliant beauty that to bear witness to his splendour made her weak at the knees. Hair like a veil of night spilled over strong, bronzed shoulders, and a muscular chest covered in strange, intricate markings. Eyes like blazing silver-blue stars regarded her with amusement, while an apologetic smile quirked the edges of his full lips.

"Forgive me, I did not mean to startle you."

Eve tucked an errant wave of gold self-consciously behind her ear and stooped to pick up her pail. "No, no," she said as she stood once more. "I did not see you." She glanced around and, with a fleeting expression of concern, realised they were alone together. "What is your name?" she ventured.

Lucifer took several steps towards her. Ignoring her question, he smiled as she backed into the well without thinking. "Do you miss Eden, Eve?"

Eve faltered. "I..." Her gaze narrowed as the memory flooded back to her. "That voice! You are the snake from the Garden," she whispered in as much horror as awe. "You were an angel?"

"I am still an angel," corrected Lucifer, "though now I am called Fallen, an outcast, like you—forever cast from God's grace."

Lucifer allowed his natural allure to radiate, a soft coercion that kissed at the periphery of Eve's conscious mind—teasing and tantalising, but not so much as to void her freewill.

"Those symbols on your flesh," she began, reaching out with hesitant fingers.

He smiled as her fingertips alighted on his skin, delicately, curiously tracing the carvings. "They are sigils of power and damnation, gifts and curses, both."

Looking up into his ethereal eyes, she tilted her head. "Why are you here? And what is your name? You did not answer me."

"Smart and beautiful," Lucifer purred, his fingers trailing through her hair. "I am Lucifer the Morningstar, King of Hell and the Dark Court…and I am here for you, my dear."

"Me?" she echoed.

"I have grand plans, you see, Eve. However, to see them realised, I need a mortal woman, a willing mother to birth a new race of being. Part Fallen and part mortal, they will be my Nephilim: the children of the sons and daughters of God."

Eve's eyes widened, a contorted array of emotions exploding across her face, each as fleeting as the last. "I am the wife of Adam," she said, both hands to her sides, balancing herself against the well. "It is God's will."

"You defied Him once before, Eve, and for it you were cast out like so much meaningless refuse. He has abandoned you and yet still demands your fealty. Why should you obey Him now? Have you lost your fighting spirit, Golden One? I was cast out for what I believed in. He has already damned you, He can do no more."

"At the end of my life, He could send me to join you, Fallen One," she quipped.

Lucifer grinned from ear to ear, revealing pointed teeth. "And would that be so very bad?"

Eve teased her inner lip between her teeth. "Perhaps not," she said.

"So then what have you got to lose, lovely? We can be as one, and together, birth an army that would stand against He who has forsaken us. You would be like unto a god, yourself—the mother of a new race not even conceived of by Him." Lucifer watched as the sparks of rebellion glowed behind Eve's green eyes, giving them the appearance of the flaming emerald stones that adorned the Throne in Heaven, and reminding him all the more of

Anael's jewel-bright eyes.

"And what of Adam? I love him and have young sons with him. I cannot abandon them."

Lucifer pulled her close until they were flesh to flesh. "I would not ask it of you. You will live out your years with your family, as your heart desires… I would but ask the use of your womb," he said, resting a hand on her belly. "And I will teach you of the carnal pleasures of my kingdom."

Eve shivered against him.

"And should the good Lord choose to send you to my dark gates, know that you will be received with open arms. Hell would be your haven of desire, and plenty. I would crown you before the Dark Court as a queen, and the mother of my children. What say you, Eve? Will you indulge your curiosity and wickedness for me?"

Eve pursed her lips in thought, glancing around again—ensuring they were alone, and out of sight of Adam as he laboured. And Lucifer knew that he had won.

"I will," she answered, both empowered and afraid. "I have given birth twice, Lucifer, to my sons Cain and Abel. If I am to give life to these children of ours, how will I survive it? God's curse is upon me. Birthing is a pain unlike any that man could ever know. I could not birth an army… I would surely die. My body could not endure such a feat."

Lucifer's hands trailed up and down her spine, before both came to rest on her generous hips. "You need not fear the pain of birth, or discovery, my golden beauty. I have spawned children with Lilith, and whilst she is now a demon, she was once mortal: the first woman, in fact. Due to the nature of my angelic blood, I have discovered that any child of mine forms in an intangible manner. The child manifests only in spirit, within the womb, but takes corporeal flesh at will beyond gestation."

"So…Adam will not know that I bear your seed? He will never bear witness to the pregnancy?"

"It is so," Lucifer confirmed, an errant hand cupping and kneading a pert breast. "One of my many gifts is that of prescience. I can see what is to be before it happens. Our Nephilim will be akin to my demon offspring, but unique. They will be Realmwalkers, children of flesh and spirit that can walk both on Earth and in Hell, at will. They will have more freedom than my demons, they may come and go as they please, taking whichever form they so desire. My demons are bound to Hell and can only cross the divide with my blessing. Our children, Eve, will not be so beholden."

"How will I know when it is time?" she asked. "If there is no physical birth?"

"Blood sings to blood. You will feel the darkling spirit leave you, and it will come to me, to be raised in Hell. I need only for you to care for yourself, so that the flesh of our children is strong, and for you to give yourself to me, as often as I need."

Eve licked her lips as she gazed up into Lucifer's eyes. "When will we…?" she trailed off.

The Fallen Angel raised a glamour to conceal their presence as he laid her down upon the clover by the well. "Let me show you pleasures of which Adam knows nothing."

***

In the distance, Adam returned to his modest homestead, dragging a slain beast behind him. His hunt had been successful, and they would have meat enough to last the family two moons. Entering their small hut, he scratched his head, finding his sons huddled alone by the central hearth fire.

"Where is your mother?" he asked.

The eldest, Cain, answered, "We have not seen her since the sun was at its peak. She went to fetch water, for making supper, and has not returned from the well. We did our chores, father, and by the time we came in, we dared not go looking for her. You told us to mind the well."

Adam's brow furrowed, and he grimaced. Something wasn't right. It was unlike Eve to wander or fail to complete her duties as a wife. "Stay. It's dark now, and the creatures of the night roam. I will return with your mother as soon as I find her." Leaving the carcass, he ventured out into the evening, only for Eve to stumble into him, knocking them both back into the light of their home.

"Eve, where have you been, are you hurt?"

Adam's wife flushed a telltale shade of red, ducking her face from his sight as she tucked her golden hair behind her ear.

The line of Adam's lip hardened as he watched his wife busy herself with their children. He could not help but feel suspicion and jealousy rise within him. Eve's silence was damning.

Envy

Author Biographies

Envy

ANDREA EAKER

Andrea Eaker lives in the Seattle area, and works as a researcher in the aviation industry. She loves coffee, theatre, and the overcast days of the Pacific Northwest that give her an excuse to stay inside and write. Her stories have appeared in Blue Fifth Review, Shooter Literary Magazine, and Every Day Fiction.

CLINT FOSTER

Clint Foster lives with his herd of four cats, beloved Basset, Zero, and wonderful wife, Nik. He loves to tell stories just as much as he loves to read them and is excited to share his work. A long time consumer of media of all kinds, he enjoys giving back what he hopes everyone else thinks are good stories.

Facebook: ClintFosterAuthor

DAVID GREEN

David Green is a writer based in Co Galway, Ireland. Growing up between there and Manchester, UK meant David rarely saw sunlight in his childhood, which has no doubt had an effect on his dark writings. Published in places such as Nymphs, Nocturnal Sires and previous Black Hare Press anthologies, David is aiming to release his debut novel in 2020.

Twitter: @DavidGreenWrite
Website: davidgreenwritercom.wordpress.com

DESTINY EVE PIFER

Destiny Eve Pifer is a published author whose work has appeared in numerous anthologies and magazines. Her stories have been featured in FATE Magazine, True Confessions, Spotlight on Recovery and Country Magazine. A lover of all things supernatural and spooky she resides in Punxsutawney, Pennsylvania with her son Dartanyan.

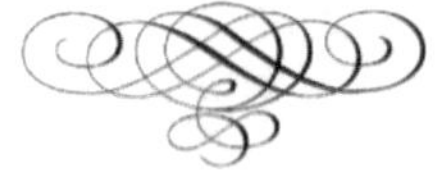

FRANCES TATE

Frances Tate is a British self-published writer of vampires and drabbles who lives in the north west of England. She enjoys gardening, exploring historical sites, cinema, reading and travelling. She's taken pleasure in flight-planning a cabbage white butterfly approach to careers, preferring to generalise rather than specialise. She trained as an Economics high school teacher and has a private pilot's licence amongst other things. Currently she writes (very restrained) overhaul instructions for an engineering company.

Twitter: @tate_writes

J.W. GARRETT

J.W. Garrett has been writing in one form or another since she was a teenager. She writes speculative fiction from the sunny beaches of Florida, but loves the mountains of Virginia where she was born. Her writings include novels as well as short stories and poetry. Since completing Remeon's Crusade, the third book in her sci-fi fantasy series, Realms of Chaos, she has been hard at work on the next installment, scheduled to release in 2021. When she's not hanging out with her characters, her favorite activities are reading, running and spending time with family.

Website: jwgarrett.com
BHC Press: Author_JW_Garrett

JAMES LIPSON

James Lipson's debut book, Fallen and Other Stories, was published in 2019. His short stories have appeared in Black Hare Press Anthologies, Zombie Pirate Publishing, Clarendon Publishing Anthologies, Teleport Magazine and others. With a background in art, James has naturally turned to illustrating as he writes, bringing many of his short stories to life not only with descriptive detail, but also detailed visual imagery.

Website: www.jameslipson.com
Instagram: jameslipsonart

JESSICA CHANESE

Jessica Chanese is a speculative fiction writer living in Upstate New York with her husband, two children, and two dogs. Her short stories have been featured in Black Hare Press' Lust anthology, Verse of Silence literary magazine, and Cloaked Press' forthcoming Fall into Fantasy anthology. She is also working diligently to find a path to publishing for her quirky contemporary fantasy novel starring a suburban mom, a minivan, and demons.

Website: www.jessicachanesewrites.com
Twitter: @jchanese

JO NIEDERHOFF

Jo Niederhoff is a fantasy writer from Aurora, Colorado who was very glad to return to the mountains after four years studying writing in Galesburg, Illinois. When she's not writing, she corrals multiple small children and acts in various community theater productions. Her work has previously appeared in Fierce Tales: Shadow Realms, published by Millhaven Press.

Twitter: @joniederhoff

JODI JENSEN

Jodi Jensen, author of time travel romances and speculative fiction short stories, grew up moving from California, to Massachusetts, and a few other places in between, before finally settling in Utah at the ripe old age of nine. The nomadic life fed her sense of adventure as a child and the wanderlust continues to this day. With a passion for old cemeteries, historical buildings and sweeping sagas of days gone by, it was only natural she'd dream of time traveling to all the places that sparked her imagination.

Twitter: @WritesJodi
Facebook: jodijensenwrites

K.B. ELIJAH

K.B. Elijah is a fantasy author living in Brisbane, Australia with her husband and three cockatiels. A lawyer by day, and a writer by...also day, because she needs her solid nine hours of sleep per night (not that the cockatiels let her sleep past 6am). K.B. writes for various international anthologies, and her work features in dozens of collections about the mysterious, the magical and the macabre. Her own books of short fantasy novellas with twists, The Empty Sky and Out of the Nowhere, are available on paperback and Kindle now.

Website: www.kbelijah.com
Instagram: k.b.elijah

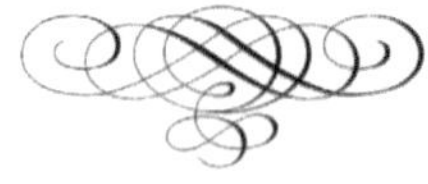

KAITLYN LYNCH

Kaitlyn Lynch is an actor, director, and author of dark fiction. She is the founder of non-profit theatre company Door 14 Productions and represents Author Services with KMP Entertainment. Her work is forthcoming in anthologies from Blood Song Books and Alternating Current Press, and with Ghostlight & The Weird and Whatnot magazines. With Turkish-Italian-Ashkenazi roots and a Christian upbringing, she has a strong and unique cultural identity that shapes the narrative voice of her writing. Lynch lives in the Chicagoland area and is earning her BFA in Creative Writing through Full Sail University.

Twitter: @mekaitlynlynch
Website: kaitlynlynch.com

KELLY MATSUURA

Kelly Matsuura writes diverse YA, fantasy, and literary fiction. She is the creator of The Insignia Series' anthologies (Asian fantasy themed) and has had stories published with Ink & Locket Press, A Murder of Storytellers, Black Hare Press, and many more. Kelly lives in Nagoya, Japan with her geeky husband. She loves traveling, knitting, cooking, and of course, reading.

Website: www.blackwingsandwhitepaper.com

LISA FOX

Lisa Fox is a pharmaceutical market researcher by day and fiction writer by night. She enjoys crafting short stories and short screenplays across genres, but her passion is for Speculative Fiction/Drama hybrids. Lisa has enjoyed having her work featured in various publications and anthologies, including Metaphorosis, Telltale Press, New Myths, Luna Station Quarterly, Fudoki, and The Satirist, among others. A resident of northern New Jersey, Lisa relishes the chaos of everyday suburban life. She and her husband Dan are kept busy by the comings and goings of their two sons and by the attention demanded by their couch-dwelling golden retriever.

Website: lisafoxiswriting.com

LYNDSEY ELLIS-HOLLOWAY

Lyndsey Ellis-Holloway is a writer from Knaresborough, UK. She writes fantasy, sci-fi, horror and dystopian stories, focussing on compelling characters and layering in myth and legend at every opportunity. Her mind is somewhat dark and twisted, and she lives in perpetual hope of owning her own Dragon someday, but for now she writes about them to fill the void... and to stop her from murdering people who annoy her. When she's not writing she spends time with her husband, her dogs and her friends enjoying activities such as walking, movies, conventions and of course writing for fun as well!

Website: theprose.com/LyndseyEH

NEEN COHEN

Neen Cohen lives in Brisbane with her partner, son and fur babies. She is a writer of LGBTQI, dark fantasy and horror short stories and has a Bachelor of Creative Industries from QUT. She can often be found writing while sitting against a tombstone or tree in any number of graveyards.

LinkTree: NeenCohen

NICOLA CURRIE

Nicola Currie is from Cambridge, UK where she works in educational publishing. She has published poetry in literary magazines, including Mslexia and Sarasvati, and short stories in various anthologies. She has also completed her first novel, which was longlisted for the Bath Children's Novel Award.

Website: writeitandweep.home.blog

NIKKITA BELL

From the mystical land of Los Angeles, California dwells Nikkita Bell, writer of words, creator of worlds, and full-time daydreamer. Nikkita is an author on the rise who seeks to welcome readers to dynamic worlds, exciting characters, and captivating stories. An artist by day and writer by night, Nikkita flourishes in creating something from nothing. From pen and paper to the keys of a computer, she has shined in the genres of fantasy, & sci-fi, mystery, and romance, and writes short stories, novels, and trilogies.

Website: www.nikkitawrites.com
Intsgram: nikkitawrites

R.S. NEVIL

R.S. Nevil is an avid reader and author. He mainly writes science fiction, while also dabbling in different types of short stories. From a small town in rural Georgia, R.S. has a Bachelors in Civil Engineering from Georgia Southern. Writing has always been a passion of his, and he hopes to one day be published. While also working his primary job at the local Nuclear Plant, R.S. spends most of his free time reading, writing, and trying to perfect his craft.

RAVEN CORINN CARLUK

Raven Corinn Carluk writes dark fantasy, paranormal romance, and anything else that catches her interest. She's authored five novels, where she explores themes of love and acceptance. Her shorter pieces, usually from her darker side, can be found in Black Hare Press anthologies, at Detritus Online, and through Alban Lake Publishers.

Twitter: @ravencorinn
Website: www.ravencorinncarluk.com

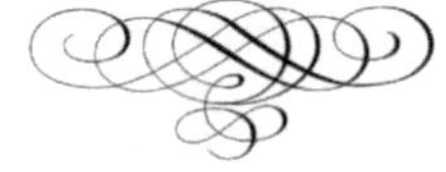

RHIANNON BIRD

Rhiannon Bird is a young aspiring author. She has a passion for words and storytelling. Rhiannon has her own quotes blog; Thoughts of a Writer. She has had 4 works published. This includes 3 short stories and 2 poems. These are published on Eskimo pie, Literary yard, Down in the Dirt Magazine and Short break fiction. She can be found on Facebook, Instagram, and Pinterest.

S.O. GREEN

S.O. Green lives in the Kingdom of Fife with husband, John. They have been published in short story anthologies by Otter Libris, Rogue Blades and Dragon Soul Press. They also won 3rd Place in the British Fantasy Society's Short Story Contest 2018 for the feminist post-Apocalypse piece, 'Travesty'. Writer, vegan, martial artist, gamer, occasionally a terrible person (but only to fictional people). They thrive on the unusual, which might explain why there are so many cats.

Website: thebasementoflove.blogspot.com
Twitter: @SOGreenWriter

STACEY JAINE MCINTOSH

Stacey Jaine McIntosh was born in Perth, Western Australia where she still resides with her husband and their four children. Although her first love has always been writing, she once toyed with being a Cartographer and subsequently holds a Diploma in Spatial Information Services. Since 2011, she has had a vast number of stories and a few poems published online as well as in various anthologies. Stacey is also the author of Solstice, Morrighan, Lost and Le Fay and she is currently working on several other projects simultaneously. When not with her family or writing she enjoys reading, photography, genealogy, history, Arthurian myths and witchcraft.

Website: www.staceyjainemcintosh.com

STEPHEN HERCZEG

Stephen Herczeg is an IT Geek based in Canberra Australia. He has been writing for over twenty years and has completed a couple of dodgy novels, sixteen feature length screenplays and numerous short stories and scripts. His horror work has featured in Sproutlings, Hells Bells, Below the Stairs, Trickster's Treats #1 and #2, Shades of Santa, Behind the Mask, Beyond the Infinite; The Body Horror Book, Anemone Enemy, Petrified Punks and Beginnings. He has also had numerous Sherlock Holmes stories published through the Belanger Books - Sherlock Holmes anthologies.

Amazon: amazon.com/-/e/B07916SQQS
Facebook: stephenherczegauthor

T.M. BROWN

Trevor Brown, who writes under the pen name T.M. Brown, serves as an officer in the U.S. Army. He currently lives in Colorado Springs, Colorado with his beautiful wife, Anna, and his two dogs, Fry and Zapp. Although Trevor has long held a passion for speculative fiction, he has only recently taken up writing for publication. T.M. Brown's first novel, The Gloam, will be published by Terror Tract in the autumn of 2020.

Facebook: RavenousShadows
Amazon: www.amazon.com/-/e/B087Z13DST

TIM MENDEES

Tim Mendees is a horror writer from Macclesfield in the North-West of England that specialises in cosmic horror and weird fiction. He has had over fifty stories accepted for publication in anthologies and magazines with publishers all over the world, and has two novellas, Miracle Growth (Black Hare Press) and Burning Reflection (Mannison Press), coming soon.
When he is not arguing with the spellchecker, Tim is a goth DJ, crustacean and cephalopod enthusiast, and the presenter of a popular web series of live video readings of his material. He currently lives in Brighton & Hove with his pet crab, Gerald, and an army of stuffed octopods.

Website: https://timmendeeswriter.wordpress.com/
You Tube: https://tinyurl.com/timmendeesyoutube
Facebook: https://www.facebook.com/goatinthemachine

V.A. VAZQUEZ

V.A. Vazquez comes from New York City where she previously worked as a theatre producer and a ghostwriter for famous fashion editors (which you wouldn't be able to tell from looking in her closet). An author of urban fantasy and comedic horror, she specializes in stories that involve women (or men or non-binary folks) romancing monsters, preferably the slimy Lovecraftian kind. She currently lives in Scotland with her husband and their wee doggo.

Website: www.vavazquez.com
Twitter: @vavazquezwrites

WONDRA VANIAN

Wondra Vanian is an American living in the United Kingdom with her Welsh husband and their army of fur babies. A writer first, Wondra is also an avid gamer, photographer, cinephile, and blogger. She has music in her blood, sleeps with the lights on, and has been known to dance naked in the moonlight. Wondra was a multiple Top-Ten finisher in the 2017 and 2018 Preditors and Editors Reader's Poll, including the Best Author category. Her story, "Halloween Night," was named a Notable Contender for the Bristol Short Story Prize in 2015.

Website: www.wondravanian.com

XIMENA ESCOBAR

Ximena is writing stories and poetry. Originally from Chile, she is the author of a translation into Spanish of the Broadway Musical "The Wizard of Oz", and of an original adaptation of the same, "Navidad en Oz", both produced in her home country. Since 2018 she has published several short stories in various anthologies and online platforms, and is now slowly working on her own collection. Ximena has a degree in Arts & Communication Science and lives in Nottingham with her family.

Facebook: Ximenautora
Twitter: @laximenin

ZOEY XOLTON

Zoey Xolton is an Australian Speculative Fiction Author. She likes to daydream, and write stories about the beautiful and improbable, the dark and fantastical, as well as the adventurous and utterly romantic!
Whether it's fairy tales, fantasy, horror, paranormal romance, urban fantasy, or science-fiction…she dabbles in it.
Zoey has featured in over 100 anthologies to date, and is currently working on progressively longer stories.
She prays you enjoy, and fall in love with the deliciously tempting tales, and the characters that she brings into the world. Writing is Zoey's guilty pleasure…perhaps reading her work will become one of yours?

Website: zoeyxolton.com

Acknowledgements

When we embarked on our Black Hare Press journey back in late 2018, we never envisioned the huge support we'd get from the writing community. We have been truly humbled by the number of submissions we've received (around 3,000 over our first eight publications!) and have loved reading every single one.

So, thank you to everyone who crafted tales just for us—from the tiny tales in our Dark Drabbles series to these sinful tales you have read here in Envy—we thank you from the bottom of our hearts.

To our families and friends, collaborators, random strangers who took pity on us, and everyone who has helped us on the way: we couldn't have done it without you.

And to you, our discerning reader, we and these talented writers did it all for you. We hope you enjoyed these tales, and if you did, don't forget to leave a review.

Thank you all—see you next time.

Love & kisses
Ben & Dean

www.blackharepress.com

www.ingramcontent.com/pod-product-compliance
Lightning Source LLC
Chambersburg PA
CBHW030711190726
48286CB00001B/271